Another Time
Book Two

Jodie M. Swanson

Copyright © 2016 Jodie M. Swanson

All rights reserved.

ISBN: 1530037492
ISBN-13: 9781530037490

DEDICATION

Special thanks to my kids,
who had to grow up without me
because I had to work.
May you know you were always in my thoughts.

CHAPTER 1

Sand moves with the wind in gentle wisps between my toes as the breeze off the water pulls at my hair. The wafting sand makes ripples like after a stone is plopped into a lake. Its coarse texture teases the small hairs on my toes and the tops of my feet as I face the surf before me. Together the aromas of both the dry and the moist granules banter my eager nose. The sand is warm and welcoming. I haven't realized how much I have missed its fragrant presence until now.

My eyes take in all before me, as if it were a cherished face long forgotten. The small swells gently pull at the granules at my toes. The beautiful beckoning blue calls my name, softly, like a caress.

I am back. I am here.

Down the beach from me are buildings that I don't recognize. My familiar wharf and stairs aren't to be found, but I don't panic. Calm fills me. The energy here fills me, and I welcome it. All of it.

Closing my eyes I lift my arms to allow the material of my shirt to be played with by the friendly breeze. The wind's fingers pluck and twist the fabric and I smile. For the first time in a long time, I can feel every sensation. All my senses have come alive. I can even taste the air as it whips and whispers whoofing noises in my ears. Every sense is heightened, all without any sense of fear.

The smells of the salty, sudsy water and sand continue to mix and mingle in my nose. So I open my eyes and allow myself another look.

Paradise again. Oh how I have missed this. This feeling, the smells, the warmth. I have missed the energy. My entire being is alive.

Gulls flap by, casting tentative glances my way. I can hear them. They are so close. Closing my eyes I can feel the burst of each wing working through the air. I am reminded of reading the book <u>Jonathan Livingston Seagull</u>. "Hello, my friends," my voice calls gently. Their continued flapping tells me they haven't left me alone out here.

Opening my eyes again, I see the distant sun lowering itself into the sea. It feels good to be here, comfortable.

The distant sound of an alarm enters my mind, but not from here. Not from this place. Somehow this seems wrong, like I shouldn't be here. But soon the warning sound dissipates and I am lost in my five senses taking over. Yet, I cannot fully shake the feeling, like I am coming home, but the wrong home.

What an odd thought.

The granules continue to float along the top side of my bare feet. The energy of the breeze and the warmth of the retiring sun fill me, lift my spirits. Sighing, I close my eyes yet again, warmed by the poignant air around me. I can feel the energy take its controlled hold of me, caress me in its gentle yet powerful grasp. I marvel at its tenderness and smile at its asking if I can feel it.

Yes.

Gentle tickling on the bottom of my feet bring my eyes back open.

The breeze has me in her grasp, and I am almost flying, moving slowly with her careful twirls up above the beach. Glancing down with a smirk, I see how high the energy has allowed me to fly.

Where are my gulls now?

Testing my invisible wings, I reach with my left

arm, all the way through my hand, to the ends of my fingers. And I go. Thinking of the controlled spin of figure skaters, my body and the energy around me make it happen. Exhilarated, the speed of the spin slows, and I stop, seeing I am now even higher. Thinking of lowering, it happens, controlled, careful, and as if I had never stopped.

My eyes pop wide open.

The soft whimper in the other room must have woken me. Or was it the dream?

Slowly it creeps away, the soft caress of the energy of the dream.

Sitting up, I check to make sure Chase is still asleep. Seeing he is, I carefully scoot from the bed and head down the hall towards the kitchen. Not bothering to turn the lights on I head to the sink and reach for a glass I keep by the sink for that purpose.

Taking a few calming swigs of water, I look out the kitchen window.

It has been a long two years since I have had a dream like that. Two long years trying to rebuild our lives and talk with family and friends and make things like it never happened. Like I never did what I had done. Chase and I were not sure we would ever get over it. I am not even sure our marriage is going to get over it.

Right after the compound incident, Chase had become withdrawn. He avoided alone time with me, and tried to prevent my time with Jay and Joanna, saying I wasn't well when the kids asked. I didn't understand him, what he was doing, or why. Then one night he blurted out that it wasn't safe for me to be alone with the kids.

"What? What is that supposed to mean?" I had challenged.

He had crossed the room to ensure the kids were out cold in their beds before he returned with a, "You hurt people, Bec. You killed people!"

I had just looked at him in shock over his words, much like I stare at my reflection now.

"*I didn't kill anyone.*"

"You were the only one there. You said it moved through you. You sound like a serial killer or something. 'I only did what the voices told me to.'" He snapped, arms flapping in unison with some vision in his mind.

Looking at him like that, and not knowing, truly not knowing what was going on in his head worried me. I didn't want to use it, the energy. I hadn't even tried since that time at the compound, not really. We had thought it had left me; Two and I had been convinced. She told me it had basically shut it off. Now I wondered if I could or should turn it on and reach into him and see what I was truly up against.

Even Kim had rarely talked with me after all that has happened. She never forgave herself for not arriving in time to save me from even going to the compound that day. I had explained time and time again in my letters to her that I would have gone there eventually, that it had all been part of the plan. Nothing I said seemed to really help, her or us. She had her guilt, and I mine.

Some history can never be mended it seems.

Unfortunately tonight's dream reinforces that sad truth.

But it's so weird to have a dream of her world after all this time. I was me there, not her. In those few moments it was clear I was alone.

What does it mean? I muse.

I haven't dreamt like that, or dreamt much in general, at all. In fact, I have rarely slept, and so dreams were non-existent.

Maybe it's nothing.

Didn't feel like nothing. Felt like I had before I knew what was going on, before I knew of the agency and experiments.

So? People do dream. Maybe this is a memory? A sign you are actually going to get some sleep? Think positive, for crying out loud.

Snorting, I catch my reflection's eye once again. With my emotions this high, I am confident that sleep won't return for a while. Knowing that my family will wake if I make too much noise, I decide to get on the computer. I sit at the little desk in the living room and wait for it to boot up.

A quick glance at the clock shows it to be 2:47. Shaking my head, I check my email. Nothing again, so I glance through some different websites. Not a normal web surfer, the mundane click, click, click has me perusing old, more meaningful files on the hard drive on the computer. One old folder sends shivers down my spine.

<u>Two</u>

That's all it says.

It's all it says, but I know everything in there, have lived it. It is the journal I wrote starting that night about two years ago. I remember the night at the table grabbing a pen and writing. Here, two years later, same little house in Stevens Point, Wisconsin, I want to reread what I started, and periodically added to.

A couple of clicks and the first file is opened and I read:

Another day. Adjusting my leather boots and get the kink out of the material, then grab my long trench coat. With a flick of my hair I pass through the small portal of my small dumpy home.

Methodically I read the lines before me, entranced. Page after page I read of the other world and of Two, my pet name for the other Rebecca I know from my dreams. I take in the dreams that I have stored in the computer's memory, like it is imbedded in mine. I can't fully believe what I have written, even though I know every word is true, every description and feeling expressed on the screen. Reading it seems futuristic, conspiracy theory, and new age all rolled into one.

So, do I really blame Chase for what he feels reading all that he and I have been through? Do I blame

Kim? The rest of our friends and family? Ours? His, they are basically phantoms of our lives, and I have none it seems. This experience has changed us all. My family doesn't really exist anymore, and his pretend I don't. I have no one.

I had her.
That was then.
I miss her. She understood.
She doesn't need me. She has Shadow.
I miss them both.
I know.

The sun peeking through the living room curtains tells me that alarm clocks will be chiming soon.

CHAPTER 2

Captain Roberts looks at the screen before him. Finally, a breakthrough. After two painstaking years of rebuilding the agency manually, file by painstaking file, page by stupid line-filled page, the endless gurus and computer systems that needed rebuilding, he has a blip on his experiment seeking radar. He slams his fist on the desktop in excitement. "A blip, but a strong one."

Roberts works the kinks out of his neck and runs his fingers through his overly thinned-out hair. The past two years have done a serious number on his reputation and career. After six plus months of investigation and interrogation, the government had concluded that it had not been an air assault on the compounds in New Mexico, and Arizona. They also confirmed that no detonation devices of any kind had been utilized. They had found several unconscious "experiment survivors" in cocoon-like film amidst the rubble found at both sites. At first it was thought there had been no survivors, but with the clearing of the debris, they had found the six in New Mexico and the nine in Arizona. Roberts doubted "survivors" was a good word. They were either lacking their normal memory and "skills," or were still comatose. All fifteen were basically a waste of government money, his time and energy, but the agency had them and was told to keep them..."Just in case." Fifteen subjects lost in one day.

Only one hadn't been accounted for.

Rebecca.

Her capture reported, and then her not being found at the New Mexico compound started new questions and more lack of answers. Roberts was sure she was the one behind the devastation at both sites, though he was unsure of how it could have been done. Though she had been coded "energy", he is certain no one currently had the ability to do what many suspected she had. He is confident she had help, and not finding Jay Strebeck after all this time had the uppers agreeing with the idea of his flight. Strebeck was considered a risk, dangerous, not to the general population, but rather to the agency, hence the government as a whole. Another person had been missing from the wreckage of the day, but little was known or on file for a Rob Jamison, so the uppers were also asking how people could come and go without their permission and know-how. It was assumed this Rob Jamison was also involved in the devastation.

Roberts shakes his head in disappointment. He wonders how these people could so easily give up other personnel's lives just for the sake of one case.

"Maybe she can influence people's minds," Roberts muttered.

"Sir?"

Roberts turns and looks at the middle-aged woman at his office door. Her tired features were a testament to the long hours the agency has had to utilize in order to get back on track, on her track.

"Yes, Sergeant Johnston?"

Her eyes are a little brighter than normal. "We have a hit, Sir."

"Yes. I saw that. I have it programmed to pop up on my screen right at first indication." Roberts smiles. "It must be her. Did you see the level on it?"

"Yes, Sir. But...there was another, I think. Same time, same place, but much smaller. It almost didn't register."

Roberts blinks. "What did you say?"

Johnston's green eyes don't twinkle, just reflect. "There are two separate emitting an energy level, actually two emitting two separate levels for the exact same time span."

Roberts looks at his screen, and pulls up the necessary information to verify what the woman said. It is indeed true. The new satellite software with all the new enhancements have registered two separate signals. It has also been able to triangulate a point of origination over the area of central Wisconsin. "She's turned to the dairy lands, has she?"

"Sir? The other signal. Could it be the other consciousness reconnecting?"

Roberts takes in Johnston for a moment, then looks back at the screen. "Hard to tell. It has been two years since we have had a signal of any kind, and the new software hasn't been able to be tried out much yet. Especially as the some of the experiments are short-circuited, so-to-speak. It might very well be that other...consciousness, as you call it. Let's just keep an eye on that aspect of it." He looks at his screen again. "But for now, let's see who we can round up to head out to America's Dairy Land and round up our lost Rebecca, shall we?"

Johnston nods her affirmation, and ducks out to start the process of lining up field officers and compiling what little they knew for briefing. This was exciting and scary all at once. Her nerves were alive with what possibilities were out there and to come. She knew she was to be able to assist in the briefing that would probably be held within the next twenty-four hours. She was well versed in this case, had been since before the devastation in New Mexico that had taken her on-again, off-again boyfriend, Rob Jamison, or whoever he really was. She couldn't believe she had been with him, or "known" him, for two years before this whole Rebecca thing. He had never given her the impression of a traitor or mole, but that was what she was being led to believe. He had seemed so genuine, and made sure she knew he wasn't ready for a long-distance relationship, nor ready to let her leave his life completely.

Until that day.

What did Rebecca do to people? Did she kill him? Did she manipulate him? Or did he help her? If he did, why? Things weren't adding up, and Anita Johnston liked for things to add up and make sense. She relied on it.

She has been with the agency for five years, and understood why it was in place, though she didn't always appreciate the way people like Maxwell had taken to "experiment" on some of the subjects, like they were part of a dog fight, and he was going to always be the spectator making the money because of them. His demise seemed harsh but in proportion to his self-centered, almost evil or torturous ways. Again she crosses herself, grateful to have been away from both compounds when the events occurred.

Johnston recalls the images she had to bear concerning the total wreckage and absolute wonder of the two compounds. She had seen the panoramic images of the sites, as well as the close-ups, especially of victims, and survivors. The measures taken to protect the other experimental persons among all the carnage were unreal and bizarre. The weird film that covered the patients had kept them perfectly safe, almost reprogramming all of them, despite the massacre around them, sometimes with some thirty feet of rubble above them. It was truly remarkable. And very scary. This wasn't the movies or some sci-fi novel. This was the real world, and part of her job. Johnston doubted science fiction writers would even believe some of the things the agency was trying to prove.

With that thought, Johnston looks at her screen before her she starts pulling up printouts and bullet statements on this case to be used in the briefing of the agents who were to be selected. She starts pulling up the most likely candidates for the mission, and categorizing and listing what other assets the agency would need for Rebecca's apprehension. Yet, in the back of her mind she wonders if she will even know what they would need to get this done right.

    Who is this Rebecca? And just how dangerous is she?

CHAPTER 3

Shadow looks wonderful as she all but races towards us. Her grin is so big it must hurt. Her belly looks enormous as she continues her fast paced goose waddle towards us. I try to not run her over as I slow so I can grab her, carefully, yet securely, and hug her. In an instant I know the presence of her fetus, and for a moment feel the awe of it take me. My hand gently touches Shadow's taut abdomen, and I feel her unborn offspring touch me in turn. Shadow's hand rests on mine, and I gaze into her face once again.

My friend! Oh how I have missed you! I can't help but hug her again.

"And I you," Shadow coos. Her tears mingle in her hair as it billows about her face. "It's been months!"

Do you think you should move like that, that fast I mean? Is that safe in your condition? My face gives off even more concern, I can tell by her rolling eyes.

"Absolutely! I am pregnant, not dying, silly!" Shadow's laugh erupts from her belly and chest. It seems her fetus is laughing with her.

"Can I please join the conversation?"

I look towards Derk with a grimace of guilt. "Of course, I am sorry. Old habits die hard." Quickly I turn and look back at my best friend of many years. "Yet it seems like no time at all since I have seen you last! How are you?"

Shadow takes my hand and smiles. "I am wonderful! I can't wait for you to see Hank again. He'll be here later this evening. He's so very nice, and very protective of me, and the baby." Shadow turns and allows Derk to take her bag. "He is sorry you couldn't stay longer for the wedding, but he understands everything."

Everything?

"Yes, everything." She laughs, and I realize how much I missed that sound. "He's so good for me. Which is good for all of us, right?" At my nod she continues, "He is patient and kind, and handsome..."

Gag me...quick!

And he's mushy and brings me flowers, she mentally snorts back.

I make strangled sounds.

"Oh, come on!" Shadow teases back.

"Hel-llooo!" Derk puts his hands on his hips.

"Sorry Hon," I offer Derk a soft smile. "It's all girly, mushy stuff anyway. You really don't want to be caught up in all that emotional dribble, do you?"

Derk reaches out to Shadow. "Good to see you too." His half-hug is purely friendly, and careful of her rotund belly-ness, as he helps her take the steps. "When is my buddy going to get here?"

"Hank had some errands to run before he joins us. Work is keeping him busy. You should know how many things there are to do before a performance. But don't worry. He said he'll get here in plenty of time." Together my best friend and my romantic interest head towards our modest abode.

No.

Home. Our nice home.

I have that now, a home. A home is where love and happiness can be found. And there is definite love and happiness in that small yet pleasant two bedroom, single bathroom, and kitchen with running water place Derk and I share. It might not be much, but much can be said for what we have.

No longer am I scrounging for food or hand-me-downs. No longer do I sleep on a newspaper mat with a single bulb for light. No longer do the fears of shuns conform my actions. I am at peace with myself and the energy around me. Because of that, Derk and I can share the small house not far from the call of the water and the gulls. I can see the surf from our little living room, and smell it from every window in the house. Despite my fear of the once warring waves and destruction it could cause, I longed to be near something familiar, and I got it. Now I have a real kitchen, simple and yellow, but with curtains that cover the windows in a lacy pattern with tulips of pastel colors. We have a meager budget for simple needs, according to Derk. But I had never lived so well.

With our simple life and simple home, he had hoped to make me a part of his permanently. Then he asked it officially. I had been so afraid, so scared when he had asked me to marry him.

I allow myself a controlled remembrance of his hand in mine as we walked along the waves at sunset, a normal custom for us almost two years now. Every day I had grown from my protective shell and began to trust him more and more. When he had offered to share his meager home with mine, I had cringed.

"I am afraid," my voice had been soft. "Are you sure?"

He had smiled. "Of course I am sure. You can't keep living in your crack in the wall. And I want you near me, permanently."

"Aren't you afraid of me in your home?"

"What? No! Why would you say that?" His look had been so incredulous.

"Because the last house I lived in I destroyed." I had looked like I was to cry right then and there, I know. I could feel the tears welling up.

But he had held me, kissed me and told me it hadn't been my fault. That he didn't worry about me and my witch-craft, as he jokingly called it. He said that he had wanted someone who had made him feel alive, and he believed that person was me. That his whole being yearned for a future with me. "Be that with your witchery, or not. Be that you cause it with your witchery, or not. I want you in my life." His eyes bored mine. "I need you in my life."

    I truly and fully had cried then. Good and proper blubbering, for sure. Embarrassed myself immensely in the mess of tears streaming down my face at those words. Words I had never thought to have heard for myself. After a lifetime of pain and hurt, I now had someone for me to love, and to love me. And to love me looking like the complete tidal wave wreck that I did with the tears and everything.

    "I need you too," I had sobbed out.

    "Will you marry me then?"

"Wha-?" A strangled sob more than a word. The heavy disbelief mixed with hope, and sprinkled with a dash of "please" all combined in that one syllable.

    "Will you marry me, my Sunshine?"

    He didn't really mean it, had been my first thought.

    Why me? was the second.

    Is this man for real? the third.

    "Yes!" the fourth, all but blurted out of my tear-streamed face.

    "Really?" He looked around a few moments. "No waves or birds bursting out in song or something? Just a 'yes'? Surprise after surprise with you." He shook his head and smiled as he took in my appearance.

    His words took a few moments of catching up to. But when I did in fact catch up, "You expected a wave, or birds bursting out in song?"

    "Well, something...yeah." He actually looked a bit disappointed.

    That wouldn't do.

    "Oh, well, in that case..." I felt the energy around me and pulled a familiar cord towards us.

    "Wait, what are you? Bec?" He seemed nervous, uncertain.

    He dared. He challenged. He knew better. That

was Lesson Three.

The gull swooped right in front of Derk and squawked a few feet from his startled face. It hovered a few moments before I thanked it, then it turned and flapped away.

His face was priceless. His eyes just followed the gull a few moments, then turned back to mine.

"Lesson number three, right? Don't challenge, or you get it? Or is that number two? You have a playful side."

I had laughed. "I guess both!"

That had been only three months ago, and now Shadow was here to see the deed done. I kept asking Derk if he was sure, if he fully understood what he was getting himself into. He would just laugh me off. Every day I would ask, and soon he was asking me if *I* was silly. Me! He was the one who was wanting to marry someone who could feel and use the energy of the things around her, to manipulate and control things. And he called me silly! He was psychotic, but hopefully in a good way. My gut told me he was, and that I could trust him.

And I do.

And I was going to marry him tomorrow. Shadow was going to be my Maid of Honor, and her husband, Hank, was Derk's Best Man. Funny how life was working out for both Shadow and me. Now we both had someone, and Shadow was going to be a mommy. That thought was wonderful and powerful in itself, but the fear of being a mom myself made the huge waves of my past seem miniscule.

Brushing aside my fears again, I look for Shadow and Derk and see that they are almost to the house. So much to do before the little ceremony tomorrow, before I become Derk's wife, and everything else that comes with the whole married bliss thing. Hustling I make my way to our little house to catch the two closest to me still talking about the things that needed to be done yet, and the few friends of Derk's who were coming. Then I hear his name.

"Wait! What? What did you say?" I choke out.

She turns to me carefully. "Your father will be coming. I received his reservation in the mail a few days ago."

For a few moments I stare numbly. "Did it say anything?"

Her head turns to the side as she takes my feelings in. "He's coming alone. His reservation was for one. It was late, but I am planning on that meaning he will make an appearance."

Derk comforts me with an arm around my now tense shoulders. "It'll be okay. It's his job to see you settled, to hand you to the man who is to protect and provide for you. It's customary and all that hoop-de-hoop."

He has no right.

Derk, now able to be part of my mental conversation, sighs heavily, "Yes, he does. I invited him. You had no one to give you away. Shadow can't be all of your past and your family."

Shadow pipes in too with that. "We didn't want you to be upset. We actually thought he'd not respond, and no one would be the wiser. And if he cared at all, he'd show. So, now we know he cares." The triumphant toss of her head has me rolling my eyes and cursing my luck in having her as my best friend.

Derk squeezes my shoulders again, comforting. "Yes, he cares, and is coming. It is a good thing. Trust me. Let the past be in the past." He looks deep in my nervous eyes, and I get lost in his, the peace and love there. "Please."

Carefully realizing I have no choice in this trap that has been set, I slowly nod. "He better behave himself."

"In two years, not one misstep from him. No malice or contempt."

No nothing, Derk. No news, no caring. Nothing.

"Peace, Bec. It'll be okay. If it's not, you can make him so he's not here, and no one will be the wiser." Shadow taunts with a knowing smile. "I don't think it'll be necessary, but just in case, we have agreed to let you straighten him out if need be. Privately, of course."

My eyes dart to the two conspirators before me. I had been so happy about my wedding day coming, and now the sense of doom and anger filled my vision of what is supposed to be my special day.

"He better be civil."

Shadow tosses back, "If you are, he will be."

I toss her a look of innocence and threat all in one. For some reason she thinks it's funny. Again her whole body and bulge ripple in laughter.

Doesn't anyone take me serious anymore?

CHAPTER 4

"Mommy?"

My eyes pop open, trying to focus on where the voice had just come from. My nearly nine year old son looks at me with a weird look on his face. Struggling against the heavy weight of my lethargic body I work myself into a half-awake position. "Hey Dude. What's up?"

"Are we going to have a birthday party for me, or not?"

His question throws me way off. I struggle to sit upright. Blinking back the tiredness, I refocus on my son's face. "Sure, I think we can manage that. You have some friends you want to have come over?" His eager nod brings a smile to my face. "Okay. How many are you wanting at this party of yours?"

He starts rattling off names and I realize I have lost count already. Patiently he renames them when I prompt him to restart for me.

"Uhm...Jay? That's like...fifteen people." I don't let on that one is a girl, and now I know who his crush is. How cute, his first real crush. "I don't know if we can fit that many people here."

His face looks defeated. "Oh. Okay. I just thought I'd ask."

His disappointment burns me. "I didn't say 'no'. I just said I didn't know if we could fit that many people here at our little house. I can try to see what your dad says. Maybe we can try and find a place to have your party, you know like at Pizza Hut or Burger King or something?"

His face is now beaming and he's on to telling me potential themes for his soirée.

Sensing this tirade won't end any time soon, I push him out of my way and sit up the rest of the way. "Come on, Little Man. We need to get you off to school. I'll try to get something worked out for you. I have a couple of weeks, and I have to see when Daddy has off." As he leaves to get ready, I hope he didn't notice my wince when mentioning "Daddy."

Twenty minutes later we're in our car heading off to school; the kids bickering about who gets to sit where and who has more friends and why. I am zoned out, not really listening. I have a strange feeling, a panic almost. Hard to place it, but it almost feels like what I have heard an anxiety attack feels like.

Time seems to be a bit jumpy and disconnected today.

After just a few minutes, we are at the front of the school, and after wishing the kids a quick, "Have a great day!" I start towards Wal-Mart so Chase, or I should really be calling him Mitch, and I can talk about this party. We haven't really done anything since we moved here, since that day I came home and our lives were changed forever.

Maybe this will help.

It could help.

"Hi Tanya!" a "friendly" voice calls as I enter the familiar confines of our local Wal-Mart.

My heart stops. That anxiety again, that sense of panic. Swallowing it, I smile towards the greeter. "Hi Michelle. Know where I can find...Mitch?" Two years and it hasn't gotten any easier.

"Uhm...yeah. He's stocking near Christmas," she offers, her eyes never leaving mine. "Not shopping then today?"

She noticed my lack of cart. Observant, but I knew how her eyes didn't hold the light of her voice. I knew she looked at my husband like he was some chocolate covered dessert with whipped cream, cherries, and sprinkles set before her. "Nah. Just have to ask him something about our son's birthday. Thanks."

But Michelle is already talking to someone else bee-bopping through her doors. Lucky she can feel so carefree and at ease with people.

I used to be like that, I mentally target myself. *Used to go places, do things, see friends.*

Shaking my head I head towards the Christmas World that had begun to fill the East part of the store. Trees lit up the area and lawn ornaments offered seasonal cheer I didn't feel. Spying him with a manager, I settle on browsing while I wait. Usually my husband worked a different shift, but with all the holiday rumpus and hype, he had been asked to be more flexible. He had readily agreed.

Anything to keep away from me.

After strolling along through the aisles I finally focus on where I am. Alarm clocks crowd me from both sides. The dream two nights ago comes back to me in an instant, as well as the reading of my journal until the alarm clocks had sounded in the previously silent air. It had seemed odd, like the foreshadowing I had been learning about in my college classes.

"You need something?"

Chase's voice is dead, without emotion, and I prepare to face his equally vacant face. I poise a careful smile before I turn. "Hi. Uhm...we need to talk about...Dude's birthday party. About us. About a lot of things. I can't keep doing this." He looks away as I continue. "Pretending to be with me, but rushing to be away from me isn't going make this right."

He raises his eyebrows and continues to look away. "This is not the time or place...*Tanya*," he all but snarls out. "I have work to do. Let's talk about it when I get home." Chase turns to leave.

"When will that be?" I challenge. "I never see

you. You never are home when I am. Never around to talk to...or with. It's not right."

"Not right?" That's his snorted reply. He comes in close and snarls low, "You aren't right. Look at what you have done, and tell me you are right."

"Why are you doing this?" Tears fill my eyes.

"Because we aren't 'we' anymore. 'We' haven't been. I can't do this, not with you...anymore." He starts walking. I cannot stop him.

The nearby alarm clocks have the only faces that see my tears fall as I stand watching him go.

Work seems so out of whack, or maybe it is still me. I can't seem to focus on the orders coming through the headphones from the drive-thru patrons. For three hours I've had to ask people repeat which combo number, which condiments they did and didn't want, and have them get just as frustrated with me in return. Despite my myriad apologies, I knew the manager would pull me aside soon to talk with me about my "behavior." He probably couldn't wait for the last of the rush to be over to have some words about my issues working an area I usually excel at. That thought only makes me more upset.

The person at the window takes my apology with a kind smile. He's been here before, a regular. His name is Bill something, and always "No tomatoes." Today, I can't seem to even get that right. As he pulls away, his watch chimes in its alarm noting noon, and he hits the button. Same thing I have seen him do many times, but this time I really notice it.

"Sorry," I offer again. "See you next time."

The briefing hadn't taken as long as Roberts had thought. Already he has dispatched a pair of his remaining finest, Agents Trevor Samuels and Aaron Tafton, to central Wisconsin to intercept the elusive Rebecca. They had the help now of some undercover agents from the FBI, which

Roberts hadn't been sure he was going to be able to finagle. As it was now, a total team effort of fourteen were en route to the guessed location of Rebecca's runaway family.

"Time is running out for you."

CHAPTER 5

Seeing Jay sitting on his couch in his living room as he takes in the local news makes me second guess my being here. Knowing his buddy Mike Drake will probably be over shortly for Monday Night Football, I rap on his door. Jay quickly checks his clock and then sees me at the window by his front door.

"Well, if this isn't a surprise. How are you?" Jay smiles and holds the door open for me to pass.

"Awful." Feeling his eyes on me, I continue, "He's leaving me. He says he can't do this anymore. That he can't live with a murderer, or freak anymore. He says he's going to fight for custody of Jay and Joanna too." The tears are rolling down my face as I blubber on, "He says that he's already filed for divorce and has been waiting for the right moment to 'serve' me. I have no one. I have nothing! What the hell did I fight for then? Huh? Why did I try to end this running two years ago, only to have this happen?" Jay slowly closes the door behind me and ushers me to have a seat on his couch. "I cannot believe he's doing this."

Jay takes a long moment before he speaks. "Not everyone can understand this kind of thing. I didn't do well at this with Angela. I flubbed up big time. I said things I didn't mean, that weren't true. Maybe he's still just venting?"

Angrily I shake my head. "Here." I pull out the stack of papers from my purse. "I have been served. He wants full custody and for me to have chaperoned visitation! He says I am a danger to my kids!" Trying to keep from crying, I find myself almost shouting with hysterics. "He says I'm dangerous!" The sobs come in full force now, and I swipe at my face.

Jay's hand tries to calm my flailing hands. "Bec. Calm down. He isn't going to get the kids. We all know that. You haven't even had dreams in almost two years. You haven't even been able to recreate the stuff we did in those few sessions with Gabe. He might still be freaked out by everything, and frankly I don't blame him. Do you? I mean, really? Especially after everything that has happened? All that has had to change?" I only look into Jay's face as he continues. "He's had to rework a family, find a new job, a new means to take care of everyone, learn a new identity..."

"So have I! So have you. So have the kids. He's not the only one!" My pitched voice resounds in his small living room.

"I know, you know. I am sure deep down he knows too. Maybe it's just been too much." Jay offers a napkin off his stack near the chips for the game. "He's had a harder road in his mind. He can't see it through your eyes, only his."

My eyes seek his. "He's already come to you on this hasn't he?" I accuse.

Jay sighs and rubs his face as he heads back to his chair. "Chase and I have talked on this issue a number of times. I had advised him, based on my personal experience, to seek counseling and wait it out, and definitely that he needed to talk with you about everything."

I listen as Jay talks about all the things Chase could not seem to share with me. Hearing someone else tell me Chase's concerns and desires and frustrations really hurt, but I know Jay wasn't one to lash out at. He is a true friend of the family, especially having given up all that he did for us. But having Chase trust Jay more than me tore me apart. Having Chase's voice come out as Jay's telling me his anguishes and own nightmares becomes more and more bitter to take, yet I try for some therapeutic sense of understanding. I don't even hear Mike come in as Jay continues talking to me, sharing everything he feels he can, and adding in his own experience and insights with Angela and having witnessed our family over the past two years.

"I just thought as he had given this this much time, that he'd come to share this with you." Jay shakes his head. "I was wrong. But if this is his decision, I hope you now understand it."

Numbly, I nod.

"Don't worry about the custody thing too much. He really doesn't have much to stand on and the courts will want to see why he is adamant about it. He can't go into it, so it is just a scare tactic. He loves his kids and thinks he is doing what he feels is best."

Numbly, I nod.

Jay takes my hand and squeezes it gently. "Are you okay?"

A question comes to numb, mumbling mind. "Why even get a divorce? We aren't really who the forged license says we are."

Rubbing his face he begins. "Appearances must be followed through. You know that. You just can't expect him to be free and the rest of the world understand that." He looks at me, and adds softly, "And you were married the right way, before."

Numbly, I stare ahead. Getting up I excuse myself from their pre-game festivities, and make my way to the door.

"Bec? Are you okay?"

Numbly, I take a hold of the doorknob and turn.

Jay is now at my side. "Seriously? Are you okay? Should I call Chase?"

Numbly, I don't even face him. "No."

And I walk out the door, past the car I had driven to

his place, and keep walking.
> *Definitely not okay.*

CHAPTER 6

Again the feeling of being followed. I cannot shake this fear. It's like a loud silent scream in my ears and it is drowning out everything else. Having left Jay's yesterday evening I wonder if he and Mike were keeping tabs on me, just in case.

I know they had taken my car back home and talked to Chase about everything at half-time. They had figured I would have come back for the car, but when I didn't, they had called him. He had told them he hadn't seen me or heard from me since he had come home and handed me the paperwork announcing his desire for a divorce. When they had arrived, the three of them had watched the rest of the game at our place, waiting for me.

I didn't come home until Jay and Mike were gone, and Chase was long asleep. And still I had waited. Waited until it was near five in the morning. Silently I had checked on Chase, then to my sweet rug rats in their bunk beds. My daughter was lost in some dream world that made her smile. And my son, his soft throaty snore made me smile. Moving aside some of their toys as quietly as I could I made some space for me to lie in there, on their floor, listening to their sounds of sleep.

Sleep wasn't far off, and I was surprised by that thought but comforted.

The air is different, humid and rank, like rank bad breath. This place doesn't seem right at all. This isn't a familiar place. In an instant I am filled with panic and look around. I hear them then, my kids, screaming, and instantly my feet take flight towards them. The energy moves me quickly, so quickly, and I am comforted by its presence and calming assurance.

Hurry!

I see them, far off, and running and brief glimpses of happiness and relief at my being there. But they are still running, both of their poor bodies panting and shaking.

What is it? What is going on?

My son slows only long enough to turn and point. Carefully I allow myself to look over my shoulder as I catch up to them.

Oh my God!

The deafening roar erupts from the huge murderous dinosaur's mouth.

I slow, turn and face this foe. Now I am between it and its prey.

My children will be safe.

"Mommy! NO! Mommy!" I hear my son's voice plead.

Glancing his way I offer a quick smile and tell them to run to Daddy. That I will be okay. *Run, and don't look back!*

"No, Mommy!"

"GO!" I hurl at him. "Take her with you! Don't look back! Run! I'll be okay."

The energy tells me they are moving again to my right, heading away from this thing of terror as it bears down on me.

Come and get me! Making sure I have its full attention I head off to the left, giving my children some time, some space, some distance over this clay and sand packed, crack-filled turf. The energy gives me the speed and agility I know I wouldn't normally have. It helps bring things into focus, cracks, and rocks…anything it thinks I might be able to use to protect myself. Spying a crevice I understand will be big enough to hide me, I dive in. My breath slows instantly to not give away my location. Wish I could stop the pounding of my heart. It slams so loud in my chest, it hurts.

Where is it?

The answer is the deafening roar beside me. It has followed me to this spot. With a sick feeling, I know there is no way out but past the huge dinosaur bent on having me for dinner. My stomach sinks. My head droops to my chest in defeat and resignation.

It's okay. They're safe.

I nod, and wait, exhaling more calmly.

RROOOAAARRR! Then comes the sound of its claws gripping the stone and rock shielding me from its sight. Its breath fumigates the crevice as I hold my breath, wishing and praying it would go away. The horrible clatter and screeching of its claws on stone sets my teeth on edge. It's worse than fingernails on chalkboards, or knives on plates, or my nemesis of lack of eraser on paper. My hands go over my ears to try and block the sound.

"Mommy!" His voice is so distant.

The monster sucks in its breath and the clawing stops.

"NO!" I scream as I hurtle myself through the opening of the crevice. Pointing at my son as I run, I bark commands. "You, run! Get out of here!" I am off running, but he is coming towards me.

Save him!

The energy acknowledges my plea and I feel it leave me, rush towards him, grab him, and rush him to my arms. *Not what I had in mind.*

He's crying as he clasps his arms around my neck. "It's going to eat you!"

As I run, allowing the energy to do most of the work for me, I coax his fears and ask where his sister is. He tells me which way to go to find her, and as I continue to run, I scoop her up too. I can feel the terrible monster's breath coming hot, rancid and rambunctious.

"You two need to do what Mommy says. When I tell you to, you run! You find Daddy! You hide until it's over!" My voice loud over the rushing sound of my heart and breathing. "You do not come back for me. You take care of each other. I will be okay." They only blink at me. "Promise me."

They don't want to promise.

"Promise!" The energy moves us along just ahead of our vicious foe.

After they both pinky swear, I call to the energy again. *Take them home. Take them from this place. Don't let either of them return.* They hurtle ahead of me as if flying, the energy protecting them. Dang. It has left me to protect them. My feet feel heavy, slow, sluggish, and awkward. I hear and feel the murderous terror as it nears me with every stomping sound it makes. My heart feels like it is about to burst, my throat to rip from the strain, and my body just stops. I fall forward.

Oh no.

Quickly I flip over, and look around. It's like some class B movie where you know she's going to die, and no matter where she looks, help will never find her. It's too late. But you still find that you are watching, can't help yourself.

The dinosaur reaches me, and I have no time to scramble to safety.

Help?

"Mommy!" My son's voice pierces the night, causing me to bolt upright.

"Gees, Bec!" It's Chase, and he's holding the kids tightly. "What the hell's going on?"

My heart is still thumping and sweat continues to roll off me. I see the fear in his eyes and in those of my precious children's. Carefully I swallow the lumps of fear from the nightmare and the thought of being eaten. Shaking my head, "I...I don't..."

"Mommy saved us from the dinosaur," Jay fills in. His face is all sweaty, his pajamas soaked. He's still breathing heavy I notice.

Chase looks at his son in disbelief. "You said she needed help. She was just having one of her stupid dreams."

"No Daddy. She rescued me and Shell from the dinosaur. You needed to save her from the mean dinosaur." His face and voice, pure innocence.

"She did Daddy. It was chasing us. It was going to eat us." Joanna's face I see now is also sweat licked.

Chase looks at me. "What have you done?" Looking around in bewilderment, I have no answer. What just happened? "It wasn't one of mine. I swear, Chase. It wasn't one of mine." But he isn't listening to me. He is snatching up the protesting kids and looking at me like I am a leper. Tears begin to mingle with the sweat on my cheeks. "It wasn't one of mine."

Johnston logs onto her terminal, and stretches her neck. One look at the messages coming up on her screen, and then she does a double take. Two distinct blips, one strong, the other not so much, but it was there. Time logged started after 5am CST. This time the signals didn't just go away. This time they lasted. They lasted about ten minutes. That was a lot more than they had had a few days ago.

This time the computer scanning and tracking systems might be able to pinpoint the signal's exact location. The general vicinity of Stevens Point was a great start, but this would definitely leapfrog their efforts in recovering the individual or individuals responsible for these signals. The agents could definitely use some help narrowing down the search area.

Her phone rings. "Johnston, secure line." She listens to Roberts' question. "Yes, Sir. Both signals, just like earlier this week." Intently, she listens and scans her screen. "At o'five thirteen." A couple of clicks as she continues to listen to the earpiece. "Yes, both signals. The softer one ended a full minute prior to...yes." Some more clicks on the keyboard. "Yes, Sir. I'll update them as soon as the scan is...." She rolls her eyes at the further interruption. "Yes, Sir." She sends some information to the printer. "I'll save a printout and hardcopy..."

Again interrupted. Roberts fills her in on orders to be carried out while she writes them down. "And make sure Samuels and Tafton don't screw this up."

Anita Johnston just rolls her eyes. "Yes, Sir."

CHAPTER 7

My nerves are all strung taut as I peek through the window to watch the people find their seats. I see some of Derk's friends and his parents as they mingle and take to the limited chairs that line the small aisle I am to walk shortly. They are all dressed in pleasant clothes that speak of the joyous occasion they are about to witness. But I am not really looking at them. I have been watching for the past half-hour as people have slowly arrived and Shadow mixed and worked her special charm on all of them.
I am looking for him.
From behind this lacy curtain I hide. My face and hair daintily done to showcase my homely feminine wonders for my future husband. Shadow has taken great care to ensure every hair was in place, and my face properly painted to enhance what she called my natural beauty. Beauty I never saw, but others did, it seemed. Simple, yet beautiful.
So here I stand, waiting for my father to arrive, trying not to sweat in my linen and lace gown, on my wedding day. It would be a shame if Shadow's efforts were for naught. It really was pretty white gown. Yes, I could wear white, though extremely simple. Its purpose was to move with the wind for our outdoor ceremony, yet hold to the ideals of a typical wedding dress and the need for

customary lace. So, she had *strategically* placed lace, with more lace helping hold the willowy fabric to my tense frame.

Part of me wished Derk could see me so he could ease some of my fears, but Shadow wasn't having any of that. She had made sure all traditions and customs were being remembered. She said since even though my mom couldn't be here, she would be proud nonetheless. I didn't know of such rhymes of old and new, borrowed and blue, but Shadow insisted that it was the right thing to do.

She here I stand, still peering out from lace covered windows, waiting for Shadow to get me, wearing a white gown, with her borrowed shell necklace and a thin ring of small bluebonnets tucked into my hair holding my fiancé's mom's old lacy veil, and a new lace handkerchief, "just in case the tears start to fall." I am the epitome of tradition, if I do say so myself, as I wait.

Suddenly, her eyes dart to mine and back to a place I can't see.

He's here?

She doesn't answer. She is offering a cautious smile and heading out of my eyesight.

Moments seem to mount up as I wait for something. Some small sign, some sound, some something. My nerves and tension do nothing for this and I feel the energy come, ask.

No. Go away.

But it lingers, asking. Coaxing. Trying to make me feel better.

Please. Go away. Not today.

Filling the room with its calm force.

This is my day.

Still there, asking, tempting me with its power and grace.

Don't ruin it.

I feel lighter and cool. The dress is floating around me.

Please. Let me go. Not today, with more force.

The dress starts to settle, and the air seems less

charged. Carefully I move to seek a glance at my reflection to check to see if any damage has been done, but I don't get a chance.

"What the heck was that?" Shadow barks as she barges in the side door she was going to bring me from for my walk down the aisle.

My blank look holds no answers.

"What was all the mental screaming for? Did you honestly think I am going to let him ruin your day?" Shadow seems so angry. "Even Derk heard you and came *running* to me wondering what in tarnation was going on. He said the wind changed and...other stuff, you know...everything."

Hanging my head, I look at my bare feet in shame. "I panicked."

Her sputtering snaps my head up. "You 'panicked'?" Her face is showing her surprise and bewilderment. "You are getting cold feet?"

At first I don't understand what my bare feet have anything to do with my being panicked. Then I get it. "No. He's here, right? That's why you looked at me through the window. He came."

She just looks at me as if for the first time. Her head cocked at an angle.

"I panicked because he's here, and you left my eyesight, and I didn't know what to think. It all surrounded me so quick. I was...I am sorry. I panicked." She still has that weird look on her face. "What kind of damage did I do?"

"What did you do to your makeup and hair?" Her voice is like a whisper now.

"I haven't done anything." *Why?*

"Well, have a look." She leads the way to the mirror. My ring of bluebonnets has grown, doubled, and wove its way more through my hair. The wispy tendrils Shadow had made more of their own way, free of the handiwork done to them earlier. But my face had never looked so radiant, alive, so perfect. The work of the makeup even more refined and pristine.

Turning to look at Shadow, she laughed. "Dang Girl. You didn't need my help at all!" Laughing she leads me to the door. "And no, it wasn't your father. It was some neighbor who didn't receive an invitation and wanted to know what was going on. Geesh!"

Relief pumps through me.

Her voice cracks that relief with two words. "Never mind."

My eyes follow hers as I look through the lace. *Oh my gosh.*

Giving my hand a quick squeeze, she smiles. "Stay calm. I'll be right back to get you. We need to start. And I have to tell Derk everything is okay yet. No more freaking out or panicking. Promise. Everything is going to be alright. Count to one hundred, and I will be back."

With that she darts out the door, fast for someone seven months pregnant. Deftly intercepting my father, she smiles and coaxes him near Derk. The two men shake hands and Derk clasps my father's left shoulder in friendship.

I can feel it ask, heady and right there.

I am okay, thank you.

I feel it softly whisper itself away.

And now as I near ninety, Shadow is leading my father towards the door that I hide behind. Deep breaths to hold my panic and nervousness at bay, I wait for the door to open. When it does, it isn't Shadow.

"Hello."

He says it so calmly. He is dressed well, has taken this event of mine very seriously. The thought surprises me, and I feel...humbled. He looks handsome, composed. He even meets my eyes, and takes all of me in. "You look lovely."

Tears spring forth, and have to be put quickly in check. "Don't let me cry or Shadow will never forgive you for messing up her makeup job." It's not quite a threat, not quite a joke.

He just nods, and offers his arm. "Ready?"

Tentatively I reach out and place my hand at his

elbow. The energy there jolts me, and I can sense his looking at me through the corners of his eyes. But he is still leading me to and through the door and towards Derk.

Derk.

Almost proudly, definitely reverently, my father helps me make my way through the warm sand in my linen and lace. The sand teases the bottom of my feet to run and not walk to the man waiting, and crying, for me. I can feel every granule beneath my weight. I can feel the soft breeze tease the fabric of my gown and wisps of my hair. I hear the soft call of the gulls and gentle touch of waves on the shore. I smell the bluebonnets in my hair, mixing with the bluebonnets, daisies and lilies Shadow had matched for my bouquet. I can smell the sand and fragrances of all the people in the small chair filled area. I can hear their soft sighs, oohs and aahs, and "beautiful" at my appearance. But all I saw was Derk.

I find his face. See his brilliant smile, and his tears. And my goodness, is he a hunk.

He's crying?

"He's happy," my father whispers back as we continue forward. After a few more steps we are at our makeshift altar. With that my father offers my hand to Derk when prompted, and I look at him.

"Thank you."

Just a curt nod, so my eyes go back to Derk, and his beautifully handsome face full of tears. Carefully, I pull out my lace handkerchief. "Shadow knew I would need this today," I offer as I dab at the moisture on his handsome face.

Everyone in the small gathering chuckled, and some swipe at their own tears.

The energy moved my messy curls and teased the flowy material of my dress while someone read the words to make our lives one.

CHAPTER 8

The softly falling rain offers little solace as I keep awake tonight. I am afraid to go to sleep again, even though I am tired, simply exhausted. Last night had been a full dream sequence of Two's wedding. I felt it all, rather I observed it. I had felt her control of the energy, seen how it had manipulated her wedding up do and makeup makeover. I didn't actually feel I was her this time though. Rather, it felt like a real dream.

She had married Derk in a simple ceremony on the beach by what I understood to be her home. The sand had been her carpet as she walked the sun-warmed aisle. His tear-filled face held so much happiness and love as he had taken her hand. The vows had been simple, but powerful. Even the kiss between the new husband and wife reverberated through me with its intensity.

She had looked so beautiful. The simple gown seemed made of magic, every curve doing its job to make Two look a goddess to be worshipped. With a grimace of jealousy, I know my own wedding pictures pale beside hers. Her sun-touched hair only briefly touched here and there by the gentle breeze off the water, with tendrils in long wavy strands down her back and off her shoulders.

It had indeed been a beautiful event. Not a thing could have made it any more special, magical, I was sure.

But again, the panic keeps me awake tonight. It is the realization I had dreamt of that place, and her, even though I wasn't her. I stay in the living room for a second night, though this time on my lumpy couch. I had hoped its uncomfortable nature would prevent the dreams from finding me asleep, and so far it had definitely helped. My back was really unhappy with me, and it is only two in the morning. First the floor two nights ago when the dinosaur just about ate the kids and me, and last night in my comfy reclining chair. Something had definitely set off the dream world and the energy was trying to tell me something. Problem was, I didn't want to hear it. It has caused so many problems already, problems I was having a hard time dealing with as it was. And now with the lack of sleep, my little fast food job was suffering too.

If Chase did leave me, I would definitely need that job. That meant I would need some sleep, but I was too scared to try.

A soft moan followed by a soft whimper reach my ears, and I sit up. Poised for mommy action, I listen in case more comes. Panting and a whimper. The other child whimpers too, and I am on my way to their room before they wake their dad.

Upon entering the room, I notice the heaviness in the air. It smells hot and muggy, like it did when the dinosaur was.... My eyes flick over their faces as they sleep on their bunk beds. Joanna is wincing a little, REM holding her in her active dream. My son's face is contorted, fighting off the images he's dreaming. As one, they flip off their covers and turn to their left sides, and I freeze.

What is going on here?

They whimper softly in turn. Jay's hand reaches out a little from his top bunk position, reaching for something he needed or wanted badly. His hairline starts to show the sweat while his face shows how desperate he is to have whatever it is he wants.

Joanna suddenly reaches out in the air, her hand clutching at nothingness in her lower bunk, until she gets it. She exhales loudly, and holds her hand firmly around something.

So does Jay's.

Joanna whimpers again, then a soft, "No!"

Jay's hand pulls in closer to himself. "T-rex."

Are they in the same dream? I wonder, like I briefly did two nights ago. They had both cited to their dad about the same things I had seen when I had run from the dinosaur in a futile effort to protect them, to give them a chance to escape.

"Jay? Honey?" I place my hand on his shoulder, the one clasping his bedding tightly now. "Dude. It's Mommy."

"Mommy?" His voice is filled with relief and yet tension too.

"Where is she? I can't see her?" Joanna whimpers.

"Don't know. Mommy?" He asks, a little more afraid.

Oh my gosh. They are sharing a dream. They are in the same dream! A quick look at their faces and bodies tells me that this must be true. If they were side by side, he would be holding her hand, like he was pulling her along. Quickly I see them looking, eyes closed, for me. "I am here," I offer.

"Where?" Jay seems really scared now.

"Follow my voice. Forget the dinosaur and follow my voice. Daddy and I will protect you."

They both turn towards me, hands still gripping each other's through their dream, eyes still closed. "There you are Mommy." They are calm, eyes still closed, bodies relaxing.

"I've got you. He can't hurt you. It's okay." My eyes flit from face to face as I offer gentle reassuring touches that bring relaxed sleep-drugged smiles to their faces. "I've got you. It's okay."

That's when I heard him, Chase had been behind me and I didn't even know it. "What the heck was that all about?"

I shook my head, not even bothering to turn around,

my eyes still on my now calm and resting children.

"What did you dream up this time?" His accusation is very clear, and very unnecessary.

Tossing a straight look over my right shoulder, I meet his eyes. "This isn't me. I haven't even fallen asleep yet. I was thinking about work and heard them start to whimper." His snort irritates me, and I slowly pull myself from the rug rats now safe from a hungry prehistoric carnivore. "Let's not wake them." With that I make my way to my makeshift bed on the sofa and sit. I know he's followed, his toes cracking as he walks tells me where he is.

"You're trying to tell me you didn't do that?" His tone still the same.

"I am telling you that, yes." My eyes don't leave his flat face. "I am telling you I haven't gone to sleep, and I haven't called on any energy in the past two years, and those kids had another nightmare. This isn't me, and I would appreciate it if you would back off! I am not here hurting people. Actually, the only person I am hurting is me. I haven't really slept in two days, well this makes three, for fear it *is* me. I haven't had an episode in almost two years until the other night, and even that wasn't like it had been." Fearing my raised voice will wake the kids, I try to bring it down again. "You never thought my dreams dangerous until I went there to end it, and as I told you, I wasn't asleep for that...that stuff. It was like my sessions that Jay Strebeck had taken me to. I was alert and conscious and just allowed the energy that was pent up there some freedom. I didn't want all that destruction to happen. I just wanted us to be able to not live in fear." He hadn't left the room yet, so I continued. "I told you I had the one dream about a week ago. But I don't dream of dinosaurs. I didn't dream tonight. And I don't know how long you were standing there, but-"

"It was like they were sharing the same dream," he offers before I finish. At my nod he sits in my comfy recliner. "They kept saying that you had come into the dream and tried to save them. They said that you told them to run and find me." Chase looks at the floor as he digs his toes into the carpet before him. "When I heard the calls for you and saw them, you on the floor sleeping amidst their calls, I...I don't know. I thought you had tried to kill them in their sleep or something."

The gasp escapes my lips. "What? I would never, ever hurt them. They are my kids!"

He waves my words away without effort as he keeps talking, "Then they had come to, at the same time. Dude reached for me and told me I had to go back there and help you...or that you were going to die. I didn't know what was going on." He rubbed his tired face, then looked at me. "What is going on?"

I shrug and shake my head. "I don't know."

He sputters, "You don't know?"

"All I know is I went to sleep that night and...I don't know, I guess 'woke' would be the best word for it, 'woke' in a hot humid dream where I could hear them screaming, and found myself trying to send them away so they wouldn't be eaten by this...God it was big, this huge dinosaur. I don't dream in dinosaur Chase."

Chase looked at me a few long seconds. "Didn't you feel that energy thing?"

"Of course, but it surprised me, like from nowhere, helping me move to get away, to grab the kids and stay ahead of that thing. I was scared. I was trying to keep the kids away, going to keep the monster after me, but when I used the energy to send the kids to safety, I was left stranded. I fell." I shudder. "I was looking at the creature's mouth opening up around me just before I woke to his calling for me. I was going to die."

Chase just looked at me, then shook his head. "I don't understand this. And I don't want to be part of this anymore. I want to be done with this and your hysteria, but now the kids are involved." He stood up and shook his head again. "I think if the kids and I were gone, they'd be safe. I wouldn't have to worry you'd freak out some time and destroy us all in our sleep. Now you're telling me that in a dream you almost died, almost were eaten, trying to protect them? Which is it Bec? Are you dangerous, or are you a protector?"

I stand and take a hesitant step towards him. He gets up and moves away.

Looking at my hands, I offer them palm up. "I swear I am not dangerous. I am not here to hurt you or the kids." Tears fill my eyes, but I fight them back. "What happened two years ago...that was protecting us, too. That was protecting all those others who were being hurt by the agency. I wish a hundred times over that the others like me had survived. I wish that no one had died, only been given a taste of their own medicine." The tears fall anyway. "I wish she had done it, anyone else had done it, so you wouldn't hate me so bad, hate me so much, for trying to...protect us. I did it for us. And you're telling me it was all for nothing."

With that I sit on the lumpy sofa, tears running down my cheeks.

After several long minutes, he sighs, leaves the room, and heads to what used to be our bedroom. Once there, he shuts the door. My heart succumbs to more tears as the light goes off under the door.

I am still out. I am still alone.

CHAPTER 9

Trevor Samuels and Aaron Tafton look at their notes and smile lopsidedly as Roberts continues into the phone in intercom mode on the table before them. "That is affirmative. A second signal, independent of the original, but still originating at the same locale. So, we need you to observe the residence before we take the whole family. We are looking for any indication as to which other person in the family is causing the second signal, if it is indeed a person."

Tafton suggests going ahead with acquisition of the entire family due to the history of the family, the likelihood of occurrence in other members of the family, especially the children.

Roberts cuts into the suggestion, "Already thought of, but we need to also track the remaining members to see who has helped them, and if that person or group of persons can also be retained for processing." Another phone ringing in the background has Roberts telling the men to wait while he mutes the line. After two minutes his voice returns to the intercom. "We don't know any alias names they might be using. Remember, observe and wait for the call to come. Take notes and send in a report before you turn in every night. Any updates will be sent to both of your accounts. Any questions?"

Samuels confirms location of the hotel they are to stay at as well as the amount allotted per diem. Tafton rolls his eyes. Samuels counters, "Just want to make sure we don't have to live on PB and J while we're in the hotel. Know what I'm sayin'? Don't know how long this is goin' to take."

Roberts ends the call with the perfunctory, "Remember your flight leaves at 0740, and you should arrive to the city of Stevens Point, roughly lunch time. Have a good night, gentlemen." And the line goes dead.

Trevor Samuels lolls his head back. "Finally, thought he'd never stop ramblin' on and on." Samuels eyes his partner of twelve years. He is surprised about the intensity of Roberts' desire to find this case. Though he has read the case, he pulls it up on the laptop again anyway. "So," he tosses, "Aaron, what do ya think?"

Aaron Tafton stretches and then rubs his hands through his thinning brown hair. "I think this is another cat and mouse game. Think too much time has passed without incident for any real issue here. I mean, she hasn't exhibited anything worth noting for two years while everything was rebuilt. We haven't had a signal from a single case in two years until she lit the board back up. If this is even her." Aaron lifts up his hard copy of the file. "There are two signals now, one strong and another barely noticeable. So what? Roberts gets all jimmied up to have his job again?" He shakes his head. "Something isn't right about this."

Trevor nods. "I agree. None of the survivors, well at least the awake ones, can do anything like they did before. It's like that day every case we were monitoring lost some of their skills or whatnot. Then we have 'blimps' and the agency should be assuming it's her and now everyone will be able to do what they did before? Life is back to normal?" He looks at the screen. "How are we supposed to observe them? Just camp outside their place? This satellite imagery can monitor all that kind of stuff for us nowadays. So, what are we doin'?"

Aaron shakes his head and doesn't answer. His

buddy and partner is right. What are they doing? Why not just nab and grab the whole family? Roberts wasn't one to let someone get away, but this isn't adding up. He begins to peruse the file in front of him again.

Trevor pulls up the satellite image of the residence in question. It displays several square blocks, like normal. "Figure I can watch it for a bit if you want to shower first since we won't have a lot of time in the morning. Or I can. Whichever."

Aaron indicates he'll go first. While the warm hotel water falls, Aaron thinks over the information in his head, including his mentally going over all that they had been told during the briefing earlier. He remembers that her code was energy, and that she was someone who only had the connection to this energy and that there had been some "recall" by both sides, meaning another who she must have linked with. Of course this "recall" was a computerized answer to another signal, like a response. That hadn't been too uncommon that an energy experiment would link to another. But it was interesting that the agency didn't seem to know who or what she was linked to.

Perhaps an overseas energy person?

Aaron nods in agreement with himself. He knows other governments have similar persons they monitored who seem to have similar skills as those that had the "US Seal of Interest" as they jokingly called it within the agency. Tafton also knows that most governments weren't sharing any information that wasn't already considered within governments' "common understanding." That just meant many governments all over the world knew of persons like Rebecca who could manipulate or understand the energy they heard or felt if they were strong enough. Most people didn't even warrant the time because they weren't strong enough in their abilities to know what it really was. And most of the rest didn't understand and couldn't manipulate it, unless they had help, via government influences and tactics. But there were a few, had been only fifteen, until her acquisition making sixteen, who had been deemed worthy of bringing to either of the two hush-hush compounds where they experimented.

Aaron let the steam fill his eyesight as he contemplates hard on this. "Crap!"

He snaps the shower lever in the off position and jerks his towel around himself. Quickly he flips the door open and heads to the file he laid on his hotel bed.

"Hey! I thought I was...," Trevor let his thought drop. He knows his friend well, that pursed forehead and tense jaw line.

Aaron flips a few more pages, goes back, and flips ahead to a few others. The whole process taking less than a minute. "Damn it." It's barely a whisper among the cheap carpeted room.

Trevor just watches and waits. He sits there another five minutes while Aaron continues to flip and confirm his suspicions.

Aaron finally looks up. "When were the compounds attacked?"

Trevor tries to figure out where his partner is going with this. "About two years ago. Why? What's up?"

Aaron heads to his friend. "The date, man. What day did we lose the compounds?" At Trevor's going to the computer, Aaron blocks the move.
Trevor puts up his hands. "September 19th. Why?"

Aaron is already shaking his head back-and-forth like some who was just told his beloved dog needed to be put down. He tosses the file on his bed and pulls lightly on this thinning brown. "And the day this Rebecca, the one we are supposed to be finding? When did she arrive at the compound?"

Trevor looks at the file on his screen. He scrolls and back scrolls. "It doesn't say." Trevor shoots a glance at Aaron's pursed looks, "We're missing something here."

Aaron collapses on the bed. "Yeah. We *know* she went to the compound and is considered missing, the only survivor. We've seen her files on her apprehension, how she had disappeared, all the stuff prior to the initial acquisition, including the bogus survey she and her pal had taken to see what she knew, or thought she knew or understood."

Trevor smiles, "Had to give the agency props for that one."

Both had laughed about the "survey" the agency had procured for her and her best friend to take when they had first been tagged for her records. There were questions about dreams, friends, products. Any lunatic would be wondering what the heck kind of survey they had just taken. But, they had her answers, just before they had her.

Aaron raises his hand, keeping Trevor on task. "When did she disappear?"

Trevor checks, "End of July, reappeared in Idaho after a brief call to same friend, in early...Sep...tember." The light bulb has clicked on. "Why don't we have all the information on this one? Why didn't they have their records straight on this? Why not have her arrival date and time? What are they hiding?"

Tafton nods. "We have doctored files to work from. Roberts isn't telling us everything."

Trevor swears. "We're going in blind, under rigged documents? What the heck is goin' on here?"

"I don't know, but I think we need to careful about what we find, if it is in fact her." Aaron dons his sleepwear.

Trevor nods, "No indication of her implant goin' off, yet Roberts insists this signal we are checkin' out is hers. Why is he so adamant? Who is runnin' the agency nowadays?"

They sit in silence a moment, neither looking at the files before them, but rather taking everything in. Trevor doesn't notice on the satellite image he minimized a sedan pulling up at the residence he had been watching. But he does ask, "Do you think she's dangerous?"

Aaron throws up his hands in surrender. "If she did what I am beginning to think they think she might have..."

Trevor can't help but laugh, nervously, but still a laugh. "Hey man, seriously. It can't be that. I mean, did you just hear what you had to said. 'If she did what I am beginnin' to think they think she might have?' Come on."

The men just look at each other from their separate

hotel beds.

Trevor sighs, "No easy nab and grab, huh?"

Only silence answers him as he shuts down the laptop for the night.

CHAPTER 10

Jay and Joanna sullenly eat their dinner. Normally they are happy when we have company, even it if is only "Uncle Jay." They have already expressed their upset at having had us share their nightmares with someone, even if it was Jay Strebeck. They didn't want to talk about them at all because, as Dude pointed out, Chase and I always seem to fight and I cry. Chase and I have decided we need to talk with them about the dreams, and that our friend "Uncle Jay" was coming over shortly to hear, too. We tell them this will prevent the fighting and the need for any more tears.
But they aren't convinced, not by a landslide.
"I don't want you to be afraid of your dreams," I am telling them. "We just want you to tell all of us what you remember and stuff so you aren't so afraid."
Neither of the kids liked bedtime anymore, and I totally understood that. But to have such young hearts and minds afraid of dreamland, it was painful to witness. They tried to keep each other up at night, not wanting the bad dreams to come again. I had walked in on them sitting up in my son's bunk; both huddled together with their knees pulled under their chins. When I had asked what was up, Joanna said that they were keeping the big, bad monsters away.
"Dreams don't have to be scary," I hear myself say

as I continue. "Mine aren't always bad."

This isn't the first time I have told them this, but I know they aren't ready to believe that yet.

"Both times we have dreamt that dinosaur dream he tries to eat us, and you. It's awful," my son says. Tears well in his eyes as he looks down.

The doorbell chimes Jay Strebeck's arrival.

Hearing Chase get up, I remain with the kids at the table, sorting through the still steaming items arranged on my plate. Seeing their quick turns of their heads from the corner of my eye I look up, I see their anxiety multiply. "Don't worry, Kiddos. Jay knows almost all of mine, and it helps to talk to him. He used to do a lot of work with dreams, some of them scary, but most of them fun or beautiful."

Strebeck must have heard this, and chimes in behind me, "And your mom has some really beautiful ones. Maybe after we hear yours, she'll share some of hers."

Chase blurts, "I'd rather she didn't."

Strebeck tosses my soon to be ex-husband a look and then refocuses on my daughter as he serves himself some chicken and rice and tops it off with some green beans. "Shell, do you want to start? I bet you have some cool Barbie dreams."

She looks hesitant, then smiles. "Uh-huh. But Dude doesn't come with me to those. I get ice cream and play with butterflies and horsies." We all smile and chuckle at her brief description of her dreams. "Sometimes I try to show Dude, Daddy and Mommy, but I forget."

Jay keeps prodding, "What do you mean show?" With that he raises a teasing eyebrow and forks some rice and chicken in.

"Uhm...like show, like hittin' the remote on the TV? I try to turn it on so Mommy can see it in her dreams, but I can't. I know you helped her with her dreams. Are you gonna help me turn it on so she can see? I think she'd like the horsies." Her face looks so hopeful.

Strebeck meets my gaze, and Chase's before he starts again. "Well, I don't think there is a button to turn on. I don't see one. You're not hiding one, are you?" We all laugh at her wide-eyed shake of the head. "But, I bet you're right, your mom would like to see the horsies." He turns to my son, "And you? Are you the one with the dinosaur chasing him?"

Dude just nods, then looks at his plate, rearranging his rice into a pattern only he sees.

Carefully, I reach a hand to him, and my teasing glance has him offer a quick smile before it disappears. "Come on, Dude. You can share. You don't, I will." Ignoring Chase's sputter, I turn to our guest. "This dinosaur is huge, and a reddish-orangish thing. It has a huge head and lots of teeth."

Joanna pipes up, "He smells bad and is fast. He's sooo tall. He's like a hundred feet tall."

My son interjects, "No he's not." His look to Joanna is one given as if he wishes she'd stop talking forever.

Silence fills the room, then I break in. "Well, not quite. It's gotta be, what Dude, forty feet high?"

My son just shrugs, still working on his rice drawing, and adding some beans for grass. On his plate, I see it's the makings of a dinosaur, the chicken is the actual body of the beast, and the rice are the claws and teeth, and spikes that I had never seen. But I am not the only one who has seen it.

"Is that your scary dinosaur?" Strebeck probes. At my son's slow nod, a smile lights up his face. "You are afraid of that?" Another small slow nod. "That's not a dinosaur. That's a chicken! Just a chicken with rice instead of feathers. Poor chicken."

No one can hold that serious look on their face forever, especially with others laughing, so my son's look cracks, and he breaks into a full out laugh too.

We eat, joking about dinosaur steaks and yummy feathers. More than once I have seen Chase send me some weird looks, but I ignore them. More than once, I have sent Jay "Strebeck" Stone a look of gratitude in helping my son open up. So while I serve up warm brownies and ice cream to finish off the meal and help everyone stay in this little euphoric state, I thank my lucky stars for the day Jay Strebeck decided to help me, and my family for, what, the billionth time?

"Hello?" a man's sleepy voice answers.

"Hello Adam. You're a hard man to track down," Jay Strebeck jokes. "Had to look you up in the white pages."

"Real hard, huh?" There is a pause. "What do you want?"

"Do you still have connections with the old...agency?"

"Why?"

Jay Strebeck wipes the fatigue from his face. "Know anyone who does?"

Silence follows. "I work in a...good place. I have a good job."

"I'm sure you do. I'm not trying to get you involved in something. I was just curious." Jay taps his fingers on the countertop. "How is the family?"

"We're good." A long sigh comes through the earpiece. "Did you know ours wasn't the only one? There are those who are private."

Jay's jaw drops. "Private?"

"They pay better. So, our family is good. It's late. I gotta go." And the phone goes dead.

Placing his phone down on the receiver, Jay whispers again, "Private."

CHAPTER 11

Something wakes me, like a long forgotten question that my mind had finally solved. Derk sleeps on, unaware next to me, on our bed. A smile comes to my lips. Our bed. My husband. Someone to love me and share my life with.

But there it is again. An urgent...something. Like a voice, a plea. Soft, yet there. A whisper, *Are you there?*

Yes. I cannot help but answer this voice.

Are you the one who helped my mommy?

Who is this?

There is no recollection of hearing this voice or feeling this presence before. I rethink of all the people I have come in contact over the years. Nothing comes to mind.

Who are you? I can't help but ask.

I think we are in trouble again.

It's a child's voice. Of that I am certain, but I don't detect an age or sex. I reach out for it, to try and grasp some information, but I can tell it is already gone. That worries me. Carefully I slip from the bed so as to not wake Derk. I slip on some clothes and check he still sleeps, then duck out of the room. In the darkness of my home, I think.

The water calls to me, and I come.

"My mommy?" I play it back, but still I don't recall

helping anyone recently with kids.

The gentle swells of the waves rise and fall. The view is like watching someone's chest rise and fall with every breath he takes. Slow and steady as if that someone is asleep. For a long time I watch, mesmerized and comforted by the sleeping water.

Two people come to mind simultaneously.

Shadow! I send the mental scream, harsher than I had meant. The water ripples away from me with the effect of the effort with which I had sent the scream. For several tense moments I wait for a response. Nothing. *Shadow!* I call again, this time less potently. My heart starts pumping. The energy flows within me and I send it to seek out my friend.

Its absence leaves me weak on the beach, watching the changing, awakening water before me.

Her answer comes softly, as if stifled. *What? What's going on?*

Relief pours through me, onto the sand, and courses towards the water's edge. "Are you okay?" I say the words aloud, as if she is beside me.

I can sense her tiredness now, the energy surrounding her so I can ensure her safety. *Uhm...yeah, I guess. Why am I encased in this thing? Bec, can you get this off of me?* Her voice is still muffled, and now I understand why. I must have put an energy cocoon around her in my panic and with the amount of energy I had sent to look for her, it made sense. The cocoon I had envisioned from two years ago come to life to save my friend. It was almost funny.

Sorry. And then the energy begins to flow back to me.

What is going on?

I heard a voice, a child's voice, asking if I was the one who had helped its mommy before. It said it thought they were in trouble again. I could only think of two people.

Who is the other? She's not sounding as tired.

Exactly, my other.

Oh crap. Do you want me to come?
No, let me try and find out what I can before that. Besides we have a Baby Shower for you in a week.
And no gifts telling me what it is.

I smile at this. *Still don't want to know?* Her snort comes through loud and clear. *Okay, no surprises revealed by me.*

Her sigh of relief, then, *Hank and Derk can't tell me either! Promise me!*

I agree to that, as well as her next question to let her know as soon as I know something about the voice. Then I sever the connection between us.

The water sleeps on, and I watch it, thinking.

I hadn't dropped in on her since saying goodbye. The realization that I hadn't even dreamt of her comes as a shock. Knowing I had said my goodbyes, I guess I would have seen her still in our dreams, but I hadn't, not that I could tell.

The sand feels cool against my back as I lie back and stretch. I hadn't tried to make any contact with her in so long; I wasn't quite sure what I needed to do. And that scares me a little. As I lie there in the sand, the sound of the water, I remember slowly at first, but with building force the way it had started, the dreams, while we were asleep, and then how I had been able to do it while I refocused and meditated. It seemed almost alien how it had happened before, when then it had seemed natural, easy.

No sleep comes, no meditative state. I focus harder. Nothing. *What is going on here?*

For several more minutes I try to relax and use the energy to seek my other. Nothing happens, no flow of energy, no comprehension of what I want. It scares me. Nothing like this has happened before.

Sitting up, I see the water sleeps on.

It's rhythmic, calm and unhurried, not sensing my panic and dread.

Did getting married a few days ago alter my ability? Did my married state?

Shadow?

What now? she complains. *I was almost asleep.*
I can't get to her!
Silence.
Shadow? Are you there?
Yeah. Snotty, testy. *Try again later. I'm tired here.*

I apologize and again beak my mental tie with her. And then I wonder if I even talked with her at all. But I had felt the energy, felt the weakness earlier.

The movement of the water is hypnotizing. The slow and steady rise and falls, crest and valley, with no echo of the power there. I don't feel calm. I don't feel peace. This is different. This is...odd, even for me. I try reaching out with the energy, waiting for the familiar chill to tingle my limbs or tease my goose bumps. But nothing. Something is definitely different.

I am going crazy. With that I jump to my feet and head towards my awaiting bed. I'll try to figure this out in the morning.

And the water sleeps on.

CHAPTER 12

"Mommy? I think your dreams are prettier."

It's a simple statement, but it blows me away. Slowly I face the speaker and take in the innocent face barely visible in the living room. "What? What did you say?" I whisper back in the quiet air.

"I think your dreams are prettier?"

"Me too."

I turn a little and see my son's face just behind my daughter's. Carefully I untangle myself from the covers as I sit up. "What do you mean?" Jay sits next to my right and Joanna sits to my left and they give me a huge hug. "Whoa. Are you guys okay?"

"I'm not scared of sleeping anymore," her voice and face so sincere.

"Me either," his voice strong and calm.

"Good. But...let's back up here Munchkins. What are you talking about?"

She looks at him, and he looks at her. Then they look at me. "We got to see your dream place. But you weren't there."

Instantly I am chilled to the core, and cuddle the blankets about us. "What do you mean? You went to the water place? In a dream?" Fear of a wave and seeing what I have seen hits me, chokes me. "Why?" My daughter just holds me, then my son speaks up. "We heard you and Daddy and Uncle Jay talking about the phone call he got after dinner. You thought we were sleeping, but we could hear you." He looks into my face. "Are we in danger? Is someone after us again?"

My heart thumps loud in my chest as I seek a way to answer his question.

It was true, Jay had received a call saying something weird was happening within the agency, that people were headed our way, but no one really understood what was happening, or why? He had been told to warn us they were coming for me. Jay had told us that his one last friend, one last invisible mole within the agency, had been briefing him since the whole compound episode. And then had filled me in on the greatest news I could've ever imagined. There had been survivors, fifteen, some of them with no abilities. Some of the survivors were still in comas, and those had been the strongest, most experimented upon persons at the compounds.

Chase flinched hearing that, that people were in fact alive, had survived if they were like me. He listened as I did about the rebuilding of networks and satellites and computer programs as Strebeck talks. "They are calling it a blessing everything was wiped out. Gave them a clean slate that they could work from." All the outdated software and facilities had been renovated and updated, more advanced. More computerized and digitalized, or something like that. And with having the printed files, the hard copies, it wasn't difficult to enter every case into the new updated supercomputer now in control over every aspect of the agency's data networking.

I hadn't moved, hadn't blinked with all the information that was hitting me.

Chase asked, "But the implant is gone. They can't read what they don't have, right?"

Jay had shaken his head and said that he had only just found out that all the implants had gone silent with the event at the compound, and no one had any hope of ever seeing a signal reappear. "All except Roberts. He's a

Major now, and still pretty much in charge of a lot of the agency happenings." He continued on what little his conspirator had been able to extract.

Chase resubmitted his argument, "But how can they track what they can't see?"
Jay reminded us about the weather pattern theories and the old method of determining who was and wasn't to be part of the agency. "Remember, you are coded for energy. It makes you a lot easier to find if you have any...flair ups." His eyes bore into mine. "Anything you want to tell me?"

I glanced down in shame. I did, and Chase knew it. So I had shared Two's wedding in vivid detail. The clothing, the smells, the food, the music, her makeover. Her panic over her father's attendance and what she wore. I told him of the energy's presence for her big day, and that I missed that.

I did not miss Chase's cringe though. That was very had to miss. I think a blind person could've seen it.

I also shared my dream of almost two weeks ago, of being there at the edge of the water, the smell and feel, but that something was different. When he had asked if I had been able to feel the energy as before, and I had nodded. When he asked what had been different, I couldn't place it. No words yet come to mind.

And here I sit with my two children who have just told me that they have seen my place. "Are you sure it was *my* dream place," I try to tease. She looks at him with a wrinkled brow, and he looks straight ahead. "Why don't you tell me what you saw and I'll let you know if it my special dream place."

After a moment Jay begins, "There's a long beach...stretches out like...forever, and the sand is pretty and smells." As he talks, I envision his words. "There's like buildings or something behind the beach. But the water reaches out forever too." I could almost smell my world now. "It was night time so I went looking for you. I thought it was you in that bed. But you didn't see us and I wasn't sure you could hear us asking. Then I 'membered what you told Uncle Jay about the one who got married being the one who helped you at the place you guys were talkin' about last night, where there were survivors? And I thought this must be her. She looks like you. But she didn't really wake up. She talked in her sleep, like you said Shell and I do."

"I thought it was you, Mommy. She's pretty like you." Joanna smiles up at me. "She talks like you do too." Her nodding is echoed with his.

A vision of Two in her wedding dress, walking her sandy aisle appears in my thoughts, and I don't believe how they can even think I am as pretty as her. Still, I am not sure they have been to this place I dream of, but know that "Uncle Jay" had told us that some people could link with others subconscious, that they were coded as "Mental." Strebeck wondered if both of the kids were emitting signals, or if it was just one. And if so, which of my kids it was.

My thoughts go back to the conversation I had with Strebeck almost two years ago. The three main categories were Energy, Mental, and Other. Other had meant no specific ability, but rather high signal intakes, like receptors. So I was Energy. And one, if not two, of my kids were possibly Mental? If it weren't so serious, I could find the humor in it.

This will never end.

"Mommy? Why weren't you there? We followed your dream, but you weren't there?" My son's face in scrunched in thought.

"You followed my dream? But I wasn't dreaming. At least I don't remember any dream." Thinking back, I confirm that I hadn't been having any dream at all that I was aware of. "Maybe I was about to, and you guys woke me up before I got there?" At my son's shake of the head I offer, "Or maybe I was there real quick and left when I heard you guys coming?"

This seems to appease the two as they try to snuggle into my warm side. "Oh no you don't!" I tease in a loud whisper. "No sleeping on the couch. You have nice warm beds to sleep in. And you need to get back to them."

Daring a look at the time displaying itself on the VCR I see it is still late, or way too early. "You guys need to go back to sleep and so do I."

Between the multiple "Aw, Mom", "Please", and the "Can we sleep with you?", I finally get them back in their own beds, and shut the door.

Straightening out the mess of covers now all over the living room floor, I sigh. Part of me wonders how they, or if they, found my dream place? But a larger part of me wants to give into sleep once again. Knowing I have to get the kids to school and have to work and pick up my paycheck before starting at nine.

As if I don't have enough stress before me, I am battling time itself.

I feel the sand beneath me. Smell it before me. I don't dare open my eyes, for I am sure I know where I am. Sleep found me. Part of me is grateful. The other part is worried. What if I am being tracked? What if my kids are following me?

The soft sound of the surf makes my eyes water in memory, but still I squeeze them shut.

No. I can't be here. Don't let them follow me. I need to leave.

I gently reach out, but don't feel any energy, just normal dream stuff. Slowly, cautiously, I open my eyes.

The beach.

The gentle swells of the waves rise and fall. The view is like watching someone's chest rise and fall with every breath he takes. Slow and steady as if that someone is asleep. For a long time I watch, mesmerized and comforted by the sleeping water.

Wait, I think to myself with a sense of déjà vu. *I gotta wake up!*

CHAPTER THIRTEEEEPTEEN

Eeeept, eeeept, eeeept, eeeept, eeeept...
I can't focus, the ringing, no like...beeping in my head is freaking me out. It's been doing this for almost two hours. "Dave?" I call to my manager. "I'm sorry. I can still hear it. This headset is beeping too. Can I just work on the line instead?" At his hesitant look I plead, "Please."
Eeeept, eeeept, eeeept, eeeept, eeeept...
He shakes his head and takes the headset from me, but I can still hear the beeping even without the headset and let him know. "I still don't hear anything," he offers for probably the tenth time this shift. "You know what, Jen? Jen? Switch positions with Tanya." Quickly I wash my hands and dry them off so I can swap places with the older lady working the drive-thru side of the line.
Eeeept, eeeept, eeeept, eeeept, eeeept...
As soon as I take the new line position, the beeping quiets some, but doesn't go away. Looking onto the screen dictating what I am to make, the screen seems to beep in time with the sound in my head. The lights fluctuate with each eeeept, eeeept, eeeept I hear.
My line partner checks on me. "You okay? You are normally rocking' the drive. What's up?"
Eeeept, eeeept, eeeept, eeeept, eeeept...

"Not feeling well I guess. Keep hearing this beep, beep, beep. You all say you can't hear it, so...I don't know. Maybe I'm getting a migraine or something."

Eeeept, eeeept, eeeept, eeeept, eeeept...

"I hate those," she says as she finishes wrapping the burger and bags it. Robin is a talkative co-worker, but she gets her work done. Customers seem to like her enough, too. I try to focus on her mundane words to block out the repeating sound I wish I could shut off.

Eeeept, eeeept, eeeept, eeeept, eeeept...

"Seriously, Robin, do you not hear that?" I hand her the next few burgers for the order we are working.

She cocks her head and listens.

Eeeept, eeeept, eeeept, eeeept, eeeept...

"The only beeping I hear is the car's comin' to the drive thru." She looks at me again. "What's it sound like again?"

Eeeept, eeeept, eeeept, eeeept, eeeept...

As I stumble along trying to vocalize the sound, she asks me to mimic it.

"Oh, like an alarm clock!" She listens intently for that while I pause to look at her in disbelief. Why hadn't I thought of that? Duh! I have been wanting to shut it off, and it is so annoying. It made sense, yet it didn't. I have been noticing lots of alarm clocks lately, and feeling a bit discontented by them. My mind flips to the night not too long ago when I thought the naming of clocks intent on waking you was called an alarm clock.

Eeeept, eeeept, eeeept, eeeept, eeeept...

"Nope. Sorry, I don't hear anything. Maybe you left yours on at home? I did that once, and though I didn't think I heard it all day, I knew I had forgotten something, and when I got home, sure enough, there it was a beepin' away." She rattles on with her story and opinions. Another burger is wrapped as she talks away on this subject.

Eeeept, eeeept, eeeept, eeeept, eeeept...

Louder this time. I look up in shock and the screen is definitely wavering in and out. Trying to read the orders on the screen double my efforts to focus and drown out the sound.

"What's up with your screen?" Dave can see it too, and now my line partner notices.

Eeeept, eeeept, eeeept, eeeept, eeeept...

I can barely hear them now over the sound. "I don't know." It sounds like I have to shout it out, and they look at me with odd expressions.

"I'll have to check on it after rush," And Dave walks away.

Robin starts talking again, and I look at her. It's the movement over her shoulder that catches my eye and holds my gaze. Two men in suits, but not business class, just...suits, are waiting for their orders. The one is conversing with the other as they peruse a file held by the dark haired one.

Eeeept, eeeept, eeeept, eeeept, eeeept...

So darn loud!

"Your screen is clearing up a bit, except for that part. Luckily that's on the other board," Robin says, and I can barely hear her. But I look up at the screen, and sure enough, the pulsing is focused on two orders.

Eeeept, eeeept, eeeept, eeeept, eeeept...

I feel it, like a freight train bearing down on me. *Am I supposed to see those two men?*

The sound stops. It's quiet. Dead quiet, I can't even hear Robin rambling on. I look at the screen, trying to make my hands keep up with the orders. The two orders are brighter than the rest, not pulsing.

Are they here for me?

Eeeept, eeeept, eeeept, eeeept, eeeept...

Do they know it's me?

Blessed silence answers me.

I dart a quick glance at the men filling their drink cups. There is nothing hurried or watchful about them, or their stances. I exhale softly. They are clueless.

Thanks for the warning.

Softly the sounds of the restaurant come back to life in my ears, and my fingers seem to fly with their normal speed on the rest of the orders on my screen. I watch as their orders get bumped off the screen and the men take to some seats in a far corner. I can see them, but I don't think they noticed me. Between orders, I cast quick glances in their direction while they partake in their meals.

      Trevor Samuels and Aaron Tafton sink into their chairs, glad for a moment's peace and quiet. The flight had been rough, the rental car agency had taken long, and the drive was monotonous. Nothing to see besides patches of fields and woods until they came to Stevens Point. Neither had said much since last night's revelation about the case they were here to work. Time would soon tell what they were truly up against.

      Trevor was glad his laptop had been stowed for the drive here. Yet, when Aaron had pulled out the file when they had gotten out of the car, he didn't complain. They are here to do a job. After ordering they had taken a quick peek to see how much further they needed to go before they would find the residence in question.

      The loud "I don't know" from one of the employees had broken their silence.

      Trevor had laughed at timing and went back to looking at the file until their orders came up. Now he just wanted to eat and start their observation. He was still nervous, based on what they had discussed even today on the flight, which had been precious little. They had surmised that someone had indeed helped her, but someone in the agency was out to hurt her. Most cases weren't this way. Most were simple nab and grab, and hope they go along with the testing.

      "Fries are getting cold," Aaron's voice wakes Trevor from his daydream. Aaron glances around the burger joint in full lunch rush mode. "I guess we should try to blend in a bit more. We kinda stick out." He jabs a few fries into the ketchup and then into his mouth.

      Trevor nods in agreement while he begins to munch on his lunch.

      Aaron continues. "You know. We don't even have

occupations, since we don't know who we are dealing with. I guess we should canvas the patrons to see if she is here."

Trevor snorts, "What would be the likelihood we have lunch at the one place she is eatin' at? Come on! We don't even have a decent recent photo. All we have is the enhanced satellite imagery and pictures that are two years old. She could have dyed her hair, have contacts." He takes a swig from his straw. "Hell, we don't even know if it is her yet? Remember? That's why we have to get to the address and scope the whole thing out first."

Aaron looks around anyway and finds no one of interest, and no one finding them interesting. "Guess you're right. Besides, what would be the odds of us finding her in the first few minutes we arrive?"

Both men laugh, and don't see the witness furrowing her brow. They continue to eat, make a restroom pit stop, and pile back into their rental car.

"Excuse me, Robin, I have to use the bathroom," I offer lamely as I jump off line and grab my phone from my purse. Quickly I exit the kitchen area and am at the bathroom doors, but it's the rental car leaving the parking lot that has my true attention. It's a deep red, like maroon, and heading south.

Heading into the bathroom I pull the cell phone up by my face. My fingers quickly find Jay's number. Anxiety builds, my heart thumps wildly in my chest with every ring the phone makes in my ear. I start to fear I will have to leave a message, when he answers.

"They're here. Where I work. They didn't see me. They just left here." Silence answers me for a full five seconds, and I wonder if he's there, or already taken into some sort of custody.

"Are you sure?"

I watch the car pull onto the street, and indicate it intent to make a right turn. "Absolutely."

CHAPTER 14

While waiting for my fifteen minute break, I check the time. Once my foe, I pray for time to crawl, and give me a chance to work some non-magic magic. The "eeeept" sound no longer burns my head or thoughts as I go through the orders on the screen and other menial tasks that are part of my job description. Methodically I wipe my station clean and change out the sanitizing water in my buckets.

Dave has already talked with me to ensure I am well enough to finish my shift which will be done by four, so I wait in hiding where I work. I apologize for what I tell him I believe was the onset of a migraine. "I took a few more Tylenol, and am feeling better," I had assured him. But the knots forming in my stomach were mixing with my body's bile for a most unpleasant feeling.

Seeing Robin coming back into the kitchen area, I know it is now my time for a break. Offering her a timid smile and answering that "Yes, I am feeling much better," I take to the lobby with my cell phone. Again my fingers fly finding Strebeck's number.

"Hello. It's all okay," he begins. "I called Chase and he is picking the kids up early. You all are spending the night at my place. The kids are really excited." He pauses, "In fact, I think my name truly should be Uncle Jay."

Softly I snort, "How can you joke about stuff right now?"

His laugh throws me, "Because I have a warning system and didn't even know it." His laugh continues for a few seconds. "Seriously, what gave them away? We never got the chance to talk about that."

Licking my lips I look around the near empty lobby. "I heard an alarm clock ringing, you know, going off in my head all morning while at work." Silence greets that, and I muck on. "At first I thought it was my headset because I was to be in drive, but no one else heard it. Then I finally asked to work the line, and my screen started acting up. That's when I saw them. The two guys, holding a file, looking out of place, and...I don't know, guess I started talkin' to myself and asked if they were here for me. The alarm clock shut off. When their orders left the screen, the screen became normal. Everything was drawing my attention to them." Exhaling loudly, I ask him for more information as to what will be going on.

"Well, I'm going to have you guys spend some time here with me. Those two guys are already camped a block from your place waiting to see who lives there, I guess. Red car, like you told me, with two fellows in it. Thanks for the head's up, or I would've missed them when I went for some of your belongings."

Belongings. I cringe. I didn't want to be on the run again. That kind of life wasn't fair, to me, or the kids, or even Strebeck and Drake. And for what reason?

"How did you get in? The back door?" I check the clock on the wall to see how much time I have left.

His smile rang through the phone. "I went to your neighbor's house as if I lived there, through the backyard to your back door. Glad you gave me that key last night when we talked. I didn't think we'd need it this fast though." He sighs, "I tried to get rid of some prints and pictures that they could use against you, grabbed a couple of things for everyone and locked the place back up, and left the way I came. Those two probably thought nothing was out of the ordinary."

My mind races on for my time on the phone is short. "Is he mad?"

Jay snorts, "He'll get over it. He wants the kids to be safe, just like you, so he is willing to do whatever it takes."

"Is he mad? Does he blame me?" I feel the tears in my eyes.

Jay hesitates before he answers, "I think he's tired of running, to be honest. I know it's an awful thing to have to do, and now I think you are going to have to do it again." A pause traps us both. "I'm sorry."

"How? Everything we have is in that little place, and we don't make much. You said that your friend who helped us last time had died. How do we do this this time?" My eyes find the clock telling me I have five more minutes to figure out my life again.

"Well, I am not going to lie. It's not going to be as easy as last time."

"Like last time was easy?" My voice chokes.

"Do you have anything put away? Money-wise I mean? Or did you use it all settling here?" His voice isn't accusing, just searching for options.

My mind races. We had had seven thousand dollars plus Chase's last check deposited into some account, but I didn't know where, or if it was gone. I let Jay know that, and I can hear him writing something down. I reflect on the credit card he had handed us so long ago, saying that Chase had had that too. I know our meager jobs have helped us put some money away in an account Chase had set up for a family vacation that I now knew would never come to fruition. Even though I worked my thirty plus hours a week, I wasn't making all the ends meet. Chase had the better paying job and had been paying all the bills and utilities with our joint checking account.

Suddenly I am angry with how little control I have had on our new finances, and I feel I know how Chase had planned on leaving me. Penniless.

Jay senses my upset and offers, "Why don't I talk to Chase about the financials then? Don't worry. It'll all be alright. Don't fret. After work head to my place. All right?"

"Sure," my head spins. "Do you need me to pick up anything for dinner?" My offer is lame, but I want to help, to provide.

"Actually, I hadn't even thought...yeah! That would be great!"

Seeing my time is almost up, I hurry along, "The usual?" He responds, and adds something for Mike. "Okay. I'll see you all about four thirty." He replies in kind. "Oh, and Jay? What about the kids? Do you have enough stuff for them to use to sleep?"

The line is quiet a moment. "Well, we need to work on that, and keeping them from dreaming for a bit. Just to be on the safe side. That goes for you too, Missy."

"Oh, right."

And how are we going to manage that?

CHAPTER 15

Aaron catches himself doing a head bob, and quickly shakes his head. They had been sitting a block from the residence since lunchtime, and no one had yet been seen, coming or going. A quick check of his watch tells him it's nearing eleven. Beside him Trevor was catching some serious flies.

This day hadn't gone as planned at all. Shortly after lunch they had gone to the hotel to check in and were told they would "have to wait until 4pm." When they had mentioned this was a government reservation, but received no amiable response. Soon after they tried and succeeded in registering for the room but weren't given keys as the room wasn't going to be available for check in until the aforementioned time. When Aaron had told the not-so-helpful Front Desk Attendant that they needed a place for their bags, they were told for a fee they could hold the bags in the hotel until they arrived at four. Realizing that the half-hour they had spent petitioning had been for naught, Aaron suggested they head for the residence and take turns watching the address in question. Once they had arrived at the street, they soon realized that one of them would be looking very conspicuous sitting there on the curb watching traffic go by if the other went to the hotel to finish checking in. So, they decided to wait until there were signs of life.

And now, nearing eleven, there were still no signs of life. This hadn't gone well at all.

He'd wait another two minutes, then he'd call it a night. This wasn't a stake out, but he hadn't wanted to miss someone. There hadn't been anyone to miss though, and now he was hungry and tired.

With as little information as the agency knew, he was surprised yet again with why they were here. There were no names, no places of employment, no break downs of daily routines or future plans or trips. He groaned. "If they are gone on vacation, I'm going to really be pissed."

Two minutes passed.

Trevor jolted awake with the start of the car. "Wha-? What'd I miss?" He swiped at his face to ensure no massive drool lingered. He blinked against the lights coming on where all had been dark before.

"It's eleven. I'm going back to the hotel. I am going to take a hot shower and call it a day." He waited for the car coming down the street behind him to pass him before he pulled from the curb. As quick as the speed limit and stop signs would allow he wound his way back to the hotel. And by God, they better let him get a key now. It was after four.

Mike Drake headed by the red sedan and watched in his mirror as it pulled onto the street behind him. His hand went to the cell phone and hit redial as he continued straight a few blocks. The car had pulled off towards the hotel's direction at the first possible intersection. Mike wanted to be sure before he gave the all clear call to Jay. He made sure he wasn't being followed, and made the slow loop around the block as he had done four times previously this evening.

His mission tonight had been to occasionally cruise the blocks by Rebecca and Chase's rental property and check for any sign that the two men were leaving so "the Kirklands" could grab some belongings, the computer, and any other items that would have any indication of what

Rebecca-slash-Tanya could do. This fifth direct pass on their street had him excited when the lights had come on just before him, as well as tense. He had been careful to make sure he hadn't come by at regular intervals, traveled the street itself the whole way, or made eye contact on his other passes, but if they had really paid attention, then he was done.

But he had a story lined up, in case they had stopped to question him. He was the boyfriend called because there were men outside his girlfriend's house. He was going to call the cops. Luckily he wouldn't have to force that lie.

A final turn and a look down the now vacant street in both directions, and Mike hit the send button and drove slowly, going to make a final lap to be on the safe side. The ringing tone ends with Jay's tired greeting. "They just left. I'm going in. I'll call you when I am on my way back."

The phone goes dead, so he places it in his console so he will have his hands free for what was coming, the Drake version of a nab and grab.

No cars and no other traffic on his final pass on a side road had Mike make his turn up their street a final time. He pulled into the small driveway and shut off the lights simultaneously. Out come his rubber gloves. Without making a lot of noise that would draw attention, he heads to the house and uses the key Chase had given him.

Turning on as few lights as possible, he makes quick work of suitcases and other bags he could quickly find. The computer and all disks are quickly dispatched to the car as well as personal videos and family portraits. Drawings off the refrigerator depicting family life are next. Then a quick raid of the food stuffs produces a nearly overflowing car, and Mike likens it to the clowns piling out of the little minis in circuses. He pulls the list of items given to him from his pants pocket and mentally checks it.

Seeing one he missed, he heads to the kids' room and checks for the packet said to be hidden there. After a few searches of the bottom side of the kids' dresser, he finds what he is looking for.

Quickly righting the appearances of some items and checking that he hasn't missed anything, he ensures lights are turned off. A quick look down the street verifies no traveling witnesses to his stuffing of his car, or his departure. Locking the front door, he spies the mailbox and decides he better check it just in case.

Finding the mailman hadn't been able to stop mail for that day, Mike was glad he had double checked. Two bills, one bank statement, and four birthday cards addressed to Todd. Wouldn't the Dude, be happy? His birthday wasn't going to go 'forgotten' because of this? He tucks the mail into his shirt and hurries to the car.

As he pulls away, he sees a car traveling on a side street and holds his breath. The whole packing up of his now stuffed car had taken about thirty minutes, and he was not sure if he was in the clear or not. There was always the chance that some nosey neighbor would call the police to check out what he was doing. The car kept going, with some teenager blaring some tunes.

Luck seemed to be with him.

To be on the safe side, he took extra turns and backtracked a few times. After ten long minutes he pulled the phone from his console.

"Yeah?"

"I'm on my way back. I got everything. The mail still came today; I checked and have it with me."

Strebeck's sigh of relief is mirrored by the couple in hiding at his house. "Thanks Mike. I have a cold beer here with your name on it."

Mike smiles and chuckles, "Only one? For all that I did? Geesh!"

"When did you get greedy?" The line goes dead.

Mike just drives on and smiles. "I better get at least two."

CHAPTER 16

Derk's stern, concerned face hovers above mine. I can see it, but I know my eyelids are closed. Somehow I can see with my eyes closed. I don't know how I know this, other than I do. I cannot seem to move to check by running my fingers over my eyelids, but I know. I also know time has passed me by. The whole room is showing the light of day is almost gone from the sky. The day has passed with me never leaving the bed. But that doesn't scare me or cause me any of the concern I feel.

I cannot wake, nor am I truly asleep. I am just lying here.

I am stuck.

Fighting the urge to go back to the methodic rise and fall of the water's breathing, I focus on what Derk is saying. "You need to tell me what to do. How to help you." Oh, it's still the same stuff he has been saying since he returned from his work this afternoon. For several hours he has been a concerned man, and I have had no way to give him peace. My heart breaks knowing how lucky I am to have such a loving and understanding man in my life, and wish I could offer him some peace and insight as to what is actually going on with me. But I can't.

I am stuck.

Part of me knows I was okay, that everything is

fine. But that also is the part that wouldn't let me wake, that wouldn't let me move a single muscle. Despite the calming call of the water's soft rise and fall just beyond my ears, I try to think back to when and how this started.

I remember walking to the water. I watched the water sleeping, rather its movement like someone asleep. Before that I had been at its edge, feeling lost, like I couldn't do something. Oh, and I had talked with Shadow. About what?

The water's breathing sound calls to me, comforting and hypnotizing, intoxicating in a sense.

Focus!

What had I talked to Shadow about? The memory of her not responding, and my panic, until her voice. Her annoyance over my waking her. Relating the...hmmm, relating something that had me thinking it had been about her? What?

And there she is, now in my room talking with Derk. Her presence is uplifting, as her energy fills my room. The ability to focus on something other than the water's rhythm becomes a little easier. *Now, what is she saying?*

"But, like I said. I've never seen her like this." Her voice is clearer than Derk's, and now her face is over mine. "She seemed fine when we talked last night."

Derk's voice, but I can't make it out. It seems so far away.

"She said she was making sure I was okay, that someone had awoken her from a dream, asking her if she had helped this person's mommy."

Again his voice. *Why can't I hear him?* And I try to remember this person who had awaken me. *Nothing. A blank.*

"Dunno. Bec didn't even know. She couldn't tell if it was a boy or girl."

Why can't I hear his words?
Why can't I wake up?
Comfort him and let him know everything is going to be okay?

Shadow leans over me again, her face twisted in its confusion. "I am going to try something, Derk. But, if I should end up a vegetable like Bec is..."

Derk's shouting now. *Didn't he know she was kidding?*

"For crying out loud, I was kidding," she snaps. "I hope." And I feel her reach out to me. I see her eyes close and wince as if in pain. "Hmm, she's got a wall up or something." She opens her eyes and snaps at my husband again. "I didn't say I was giving up. For crying out loud!" She looks at my face, then closes her eyes once again. "And don't yell at a pregnant lady." She snorts at his comment. "Didn't anyone ever tell you we can be witchy? Ugh!"

It was so quiet, I almost missed it until she repeated herself? *Hello?*

Shadow?

A brief smile lights her features, but then it contorts with the effort she's emitting in trying to talk to me. *Hey there, Lady. What's the deal? What's going on in there?* Her lips haven't moved, and I know she is in.

You know, I'm not really sure. I don't remember what happened, or what you just were telling Derk. I remember the fear of something happening to you and when you didn't answer...

Her lips are moving for this now. "You wrapped me in that cocoon thing. That was weird. Please don't ever do that again." Her voice wasn't upset, but cajoling. At least I knew not to piss of the prego lady.

Okay, deal.

"So, you don't remember the voice that woke you? The one that sent you in a panic to wake me from a good night's rest?"

Not so much. Straining for a clue as to what is going on, I ask if I can get her to recap everything again for me. She obliges with a more in-depth recap than Derk had received. *The voice, I can't hear it now. I can't remember what it sounded like.*

"But more importantly is the issue of what is up

with you. Did something happen after we talked, the first time? You said stuff like something was wrong the second time?"

I couldn't...wait, something is changing. The flashback hits me like the tidal waves of my old home. The change and surge of energy echoes that tidal wave then followed by a near sun stroke feeling.

"I can feel it too," Shadow echoes. "What is it?" To my silence she continues, "What is happening?"

I open my eyes and blink the dryness away. My throat is all scratchy, "The son. Her son." My mind is racing with the voice that woke me, asking "Are you the one who helped my mommy?" I turn my neck towards Shadow see her eyes on me. "It's her son."

Her blank look is covered quickly by her relief in seeing me alert.

"You're awake." My husband's arms wrap around me, and I find myself scooted into his lap. "Dang, you scared me out of my wits."

My voice cracks like my dry lips do, "He blocked me, shut me down. Her son."

"Whose son?" Shadow prompts.

"Hers. The Other's son."

"How do you know?"

My eyes make her face. "She's in trouble, maybe...I don't know, and he didn't want me to know. Didn't think I could help. I need to find out."

Derk pushes me away long enough to look into my face. "Oh-ho no! Not if you are going to be comatose for a day or so afterward."

Shadow looks at me while Derk tries to tell me all the worry he had been suffering through upon coming home and seeing me so still, like he had when he had left in the morning. Her face is covered in a strange apprehension, *Her son? As in 'her'?*

Carefully I nod. *I think something is going on. Her son is now involved.*

How do you know he's 'involved?'

I just look into my rescuers eyes. *He was here. He*

came to seek me out.

"But why?" she insists.

At Derk's quick roll of the eyes, I know he's figured out our quiet game. "I don't know. But I think we need to help them, find a way to see what is going on, and why he came for me, and not her."

She nods. Derk rolls his eyes. Hank I see for the first time, and he's already heading out of the room shaking his head. The room seems to have a difference in opinion.

Me? I am convinced. And suddenly very hungry. "Did I miss dinner?"

More eyes roll, but I am not going to let this stop me from easing this ache I feel in most of my body. The energy soon filters itself carefully around me. Derk lets me go and heads to the door. "Let me see what I can get for you," he mutters.

Shadow still is looking at me with concern on her face. "What can it mean?"

"I am not sure. But, for certain, he found me, blocked me and the energy, and he told me he thought they were in trouble again."

"So what are you going to do?"

Sighing, "Eat. Think. Figure this out. See if I can make the connection." My eyes find hers, "That's all I can do."

CHAPTER 17

Aaron rubs his face in frustration. For three full days they have been camped out at different points at the residence they were directed to be, and nothing. A quick asking of neighbors today indicated that the family had been there the morning before they had arrived. No one even knew for sure who was living there. One neighbor had said Connor, another had said Kipling, another had said Kirkland, and so on. Gurus were running all the names. Some guesses as to who the landlord was. But nothing else was offered. He was letting the agency take care of it from that point. Let them give them some information. Not the other way around.

Now, as it neared two in the afternoon, he watches the mailman pass "their house." With a jolt he realizes that they hadn't even checked for this. Nobody had, as they didn't have a name.

"We're slipping," he tells his partner.

Trevor looks up from his laptop game of solitaire. "What do you mean?"

Aaron points to the mailman as he passes by. "Did you notice if he stopped at the house yesterday?"

Trevor shrugs, "Didn't really pay attention." Then the light starts to come on. "Should we check to see if it's empty?"

Aaron just looks at his partner.

"Okay. You or me?"

Again, just the look.

"Fine." With that Trevor opens the door and crosses the street and heads up the sidewalk towards the property they have watched in shifts for days from six in the morning until three the following morning. He offers some casual glances as he heads up towards the sidewalk. Not seeing anyone watching he opens the pull of the mailbox, and drops his head.

Aaron pulls up in the rental a few seconds later with a curse. "Do you think they saw us coming?"

Trevor shakes his head again. "Nah. Maybe we should have the agency do a mail hold or forward check for us." Seeing Aaron's approval, he brings his cell phone out. "You know, he's not going to be happy about this."

But Aaron doesn't care. He was tired of sitting around here with no information, and no people.

"Johnston, hi. This is Agent Trevor Samuels. I have an odd request." Trevor starts to give her his request, and then makes a face towards his partner. "Sure, put him on." After a brief moment, "Hello Major Roberts." He listens a second. "Well Sir, it's like our emails say. There's no sign. Even their neighbors aren't sure who they are. Some of the neighbors are even uncertain how long this couple has been here. Some say a couple of months, others say a year or so. Still waiting on that information we requested from-." Trevor rolls his eyes and glances at Aaron. "Well, what we had been about to do before you interrupted us, Major, was to have a trace done on the mail. You guys can do that -." Again a fluttering of irritated eyelids. "The mailman didn't stop today, and the mailbox is empty." He taps at the window, then nods. "Yes, we are lookin' for a name, obviously." Again he rolls his eyes and adds a shaking of his head. "Also, we are lookin' for any indication as to when they plan to return, or if there is a forwardin' address, or whatnot. Yes!" His hand slams the top of the dash before him. "Yes, we are just goin' to try and get somewhere with this while we sit on our butts in this car."

Aaron taps on the steering wheel and looks at the street before him. "Isn't he getting our emails," comes his snide comment.

Trevor smirks. "Sir? Aren't you receivin' our emails?"

Aaron casts a ticked glance at his partner's idea of comedy. "Great, thanks."

Trevor holds up his finger as he smiles back. "Well, we just wanted to be sure. We've been doin' this a while now and have nothin' else to report. I guess I'm wonderin' what you really want us to do here? I mean, if the residents are found to be on vacation, then we can hole up in the hotel for-"

Aaron blinks at the cell phone Trevor jerks, and is now holding about two feet from his ear. "Man, he has a temper. Good thing he's not an experimental type."

More loud verbiage is heard and Trevor continues to rolls his eyes, phone still held out ahead of him. He wonders if he would need more therapy to counter the constant roll of his eyes. This Roberts was really starting to annoy him. First withholding information on the Rebecca case, second having assumed that was the person they were to observe, and third was his obvious lack of professionalism. Follow that up with no help with their requests for information. Hearing the tirade near an end he brings the phone closer to his ear and waits. Finally, "We understand perfectly. We have been doin' this awhile, and we don't appreciate your tone. We're the ones givin' up our time here." He listens politely. "Yes, I know it is part of our job. You don't need to be so rude and uptight. We don't even work for you. We have to report much higher than you. Try to remember that." When he pulls the phone from his ear, he mouths, "Click."

Aaron chuckles. It was true, but he was sure Trevor was making more of an enemy than a co-worker. They did have supervisors who were above Roberts, but they had been assigned this case with Roberts. Again, it made Aaron wonder what the deal was with Roberts and the Rebecca case, and what made him so darned sure this was her signal they were tracking.

"Great," Trevor was continuing. "As long as we are all on the same page, and civil towards each other, we can all get our parts done." Eyes roll again.

Yep, definitely going to need therapy. Even Aaron can see the need and chuckles once again. He knew Trevor and he'd add the lack of Robert's military bearing and professionalism in their reports, and now Roberts would wonder if his career would be becoming stagnant. One doesn't have far to go in this field before you have to wait out rank, and for Roberts to have finally made Major...? It wasn't looking good.

"Of course, Major, as soon as we have anythin'. Now, please run this search." Trevor reads off the information again and asks for it to be verified back to ensure it was right and no legal hitches with the postal service would kick them in the butt in the future. His hand covers the mouth piece as muffles it so he can address his partner, "I have had enough."

Aaron chuckles once more. He had heard a person was to laugh some six or so times a day to live a long and healthy life. He was half way there in just one work-related phone call.

Trevor's hand uncovers the phone and he looks for his pad of paper and a pen. "I will wait if that is okay, Major. It shouldn't take too long for Sergeant Johnston to access what we are lookin' fo-". His abrupt stop draws Aaron's attention. "Kirkland, K-i-r-k-l-a-n-d, Michael and Tanya. Got it. Forwarded? Just a PO box? What number? When? Huh? That's the day we arrived in town. What time?" Trevor looks at Aaron. "Who? Michael. Okay. Run those names and have her call me back. I gotta go." With that he snaps his phone shut and looks at his partner. "Either they have some weird timing, or...I don't know what."

Aaron makes a face, "You going to clue me in here?"

Trevor taps his pen against the pad in annoyance.

"The mail was to be forwarded to a PO box..."
"Heard that." "...by a Michael Kirkland..."
"Heard that."
"...on the day we arrived..."
"Uh,huh," Aaron nods.
"While we were in the hotel trying to get a key."
Didn't see that one coming. "Let's get to the hotel. We need to start asking some more questions."

Trevor continues the pen tapping as Aaron brings the car to life and turns on the turn signal. "From the get-go there have been things, big things mind you, wrong with this." He looks at the sour face of his partner. "Did you see anyone else in the lobby that day? Or since? I have been trying to pay attention, but...I don't recall seeing her."

Aaron drives in silence, thinking. "Don't hotels have cameras?"

Trevor nods, still tapping. "How long were we arguing with that Front Desk person? About thirty minutes or so?" Seeing Aaron nod, he shakes his head. "None of this makes sense."

Aaron hisses, "How can you even say that? You just said this Michael Kirkland had filed a forward change of address while we were in the lobby trying to get a key for our room!"

"Where were they?" Trevor prompts. At the shrug he continues, "How did they know we were comin'?" Another shrug. "How would they have known it was us, or what we were here for? And how would this Michael get to the Post Office that quick?"

Aaron taps the steering wheel as he thinks. "It couldn't be just coincidence, could it? I mean, everything is all screwy with this to begin with. Where else were we?"

Trevor keeps that pen just a tapping. "We got off the airplane. Went to the car rental desk. We were talkin' about the case there." Now the pen has more use, listing places they had been.

Aaron dismisses that as he was sure no one had been around, no address had been named, and the heavy set lady behind the desk definitely did not match Rebecca's profile. But still, he contends it is worth double checking back there. "Where else?"

"We got lunch when we arrived."

Aaron nods again. "I had the file then, didn't I? We were looking at it while we waited for our food, then at the table."

Trevor shakes his head. "You did, but we didn't see anyone who looked like the profile. And no one was near us while we ate, so no one could have overheard what we were talkin' about. Pretty sure we didn't say anythin' any bystander would have made heads or tails of."

Aaron shakes his head anyway. "We'll check there again too, just to be sure." They try adding to their list. Finding the only other stop being the gas station a few blocks from the residence, they add that as well.

Trevor's pen resumes drumstick duty until they pull into the hotel. "What if it is all just coincidence Aaron?"

"Well, at least now we have a couple of names, and we have something to do instead of sitting in this blasted car." Aaron opens his door and gets out, slamming the door behind him.

CHAPTER 18

I have gone to work every day since they showed up, waiting for my paycheck to come into my checking account. I have gone to work every day since they showed up, trying to not let on to my co-workers until the finally aspects of our flight are finalized. I have gone to work every day since they showed up, afraid they will come back in.

It has been four days, and I have stuck to the back of the kitchen, asking to work the boards and line more than counter or drive-thru, just in case they come in, or someone asks me where I have been. Luckily I have no real friends and haven't gone out of my way to make my presence in this world known.

Today is payday, for me as well as Chase. So that was taken care of. There would be a little extra to help us get where we need to go. A little extra cushion to start a new life. A life that, for the time being, would still include Chase, and of course the kids.

Today I would be leaving this job and would be finding someplace else to work—at least that was the plan. My only fear was their return.

Please don't let them come back today.

But I hadn't had any alarms, and it was about three in the afternoon.

I only had to make it until four, then I could leave.

Not that I really wanted to leave. There were days I enjoyed the thrill of the fast pace, some of the regulars, and of course the idea of having a job. But, now it all came down to this last hour.

Taking in the next order on the screen I grab the meat and bun.

Eeeept, eeeept, eeeept, eeeept, eeeept....

I drop the burger I am working on and quickly look towards the counter. Dave scolds me as I quickly scan the patrons for the two faces I had seen before. Quickly I apologize to Dave and restart the burger.

Eeeept, eeeept, eeeept, eeeept, eeeept....

My screen isn't flickering yet, but the alarm clock sound has definitely put me on edge. My eyes are darting about, and I have to really listen to Robin's question. Carefully, not wanting to shout, I wince and place my ear to my shoulder. "I think my migraine is coming back." It's a lame excuse, but her clucking away on it has Dave come back over.

"Tanya? Are you okay?" he asks.

Eeeept, eeeept, eeeept, eeeept, eeeept....

"My head, I think my migraine is back."

He eyes me and looks at my flushed face. "Maybe. Maybe you're getting that flu that's going around." At my blank look he tells Robin to take over the board. "Go ahead Tanya. This is your last day anyway. Go get some rest. You look like crap."

Eeeept, eeeept, eeeept, eeeept, eeeept....

"Really?" I squeak out, not wanting to drown out the warning bells.

"It's okay. We're pretty much caught up here. You want me to call your husband to have him pick you up?" Dave has always been a good boss. Now, more than ever, with the bells and whistles sounding, I dread finding another job, knowing good bosses are hard to come by.

Eeeept, eeeept, eeeept, eeeept, eeeept....

"It's okay. I think I can drive. It's not too far." I head to the terminal to clock out. Seeing him watch me, I move slower, like I deserve to go home, but not too slow that would warrant a ride home. "Thanks again Dave. I've enjoyed working here."

"Yeah, well...you are a hard worker. If Mitch's job doesn't pan out, won't need to crawl back. I'd be happy to have you."

Eeeept, eeeept, eeeept, eeeept, eeeept....

Boy, it's getting louder.

Grabbing my keys and purse I thank him again. A quick scan of the lobby shows the two men interfering in my life aren't here. A similar scan of the parked cars doesn't produce the red sedan, so I quickly head to my vehicle.

Eeeept, eeeept, eeeept, eeeept, eeeept....

Starting my car's engine, I look at the cars on the streets nearby and double check every red one. Quickly I make my way out of the parking lot. So far, so good. I don't have too far to go. While waiting for the truck ahead of me to pull out, I check my reflection in the rearview mirror. Self-conscious, I pull the brim of my hat down a little farther.

Eeeept, eeeept, eeeept, eeeept, eeeept....

They have to be close for it to be that loud. My radio flickers in and out with static. I panic, but everything tells me not to look around and look suspicious, obvious.

Eeeept, eeeept, eeeept, eeeept, eeeept....

The truck pulls ahead on its path, and now it's my turn. Having a clear turn, I go.

Eeeept, eeeept, eeeept, eeeept, eeeept....

I check all my mirrors quickly and look briefly at the cars turning my way before they make the parking lot. I see it, the red sedan. It's stopped at a red light, left turn signal on, obviously on its way to my place of previous employment. Two men watching the building with some interest and not really me.

Eeeept, eeeept, eeeept, eeeept, eeeept....

My sigh is lost in the warning, so I don't keep watching them as I make my right turn onto the two lane road and head South. Once I am on my way, I regularly check my rearview mirror again for a few blocks until the images are too small, and I am too far away.

I grope in my purse for my cell phone, and hurriedly dial. It is answered right away. "Chase, I'm on my way." He questions my getting off work early, and I tell him about the alarm sounds again, and feigning a migraine so Dave would let me off early. "Just in time, too. Just about the same time I am leaving the parking lot, I see them about to make their turn towards the restaurant." He doesn't sound relieved, nor really interested, and I wonder if our marriage can work with him so far removed. "I'll be there shortly," I answer his question. Hearing his end disconnect, I snap my phone shut.

Aaron Tafton and Trevor Samuels look around the small fast food establishment sitting just a quick drive away. They didn't know what to expect here either. It had been another disappointing day, no doubt about it. Every place they had stopped to in the past few hours had been a dead end. Though neither of them was hungry, they decided to go ahead and hit the burger joint anyway. So, as soon as the light turned green, they could mark this off their list of places to check into.

First was the hotel, with a very helpful college kid working Front Desk who assured them that no Kirkland's worked there. Then he had tried looking up Kirkland in the phone book, but found none, which didn't really surprise Aaron or Trevor. He had even looked at the photo of Rebecca, but didn't recognize her. Yes, he had been very helpful, but still a waste of their time.

Then they had gone back to the car rental agency at the small airport a short drive away. Same great customer service and attention to detail, but same lack of useful information. Hence another waste of their time, gas, and patience.

At long last, and after many cars coming and going, the light changed. Once again the two found themselves finding a parking spot. This time the parking lot was near

Another Time

empty, so they were able to secure a spot near the south door. They quickly scan the patrons in the lobby as they enter. An elderly couple sat sharing some fries by the window. Another man was balancing a tray heaping with a sandwich, huge order of fries, large teetering drink, and a slice of pie. None fit Rebecca's profile.

The expectant look of the young lady at the cash register drew them closer. "Service two," her sing-song voice calls into the microphone mounted by her register. As soon as the two step up she offers her regular, "What can I get for you today?"

Aaron pulls out the picture of Rebecca. "Hi. We're looking for someone." Flashing the picture he continues, "Have you seen this woman?"

The name tag says Jen. "You're kidding right?" She takes in their blank looks. "Is this some kind of joke?"

Trevor shakes his head and affirms that this is not a joke, and that they are indeed looking for her. She doesn't seem convinced, like she's waiting to be called a fool. "So...you've seen her?"

"Yeah," with a little bit of sarcasm and playful attitude. "But you just missed her. She was complaining about a migraine so Dave let her go home early."

Aaron sucks in his breath and curses while Trevor's jaw drops.

Jen's not smiling now. "What? Is she in trouble or something?"

Aaron quickly recovers, "Oh, no! We're old acquaintances, friends, and been having a lot of bad luck finding her."

Jen's really not convinced. "Uh-huh. Well, Tanya didn't say anything about friends of hers coming by."

Trevor looks at Aaron, "Tanya." He looks back to the now overly suspicious Jen. "When did Tanya get off work?"

Dave walks up, witnessing the men not ordering. "Hi there fellas. What can we get you?"

Aaron has had enough and pulls out his agent identification badge. "Agent Tafton. I need to ask you a few questions about...Tanya."

"Sure, what happened. Is she okay?" His voice offers genuine concern, so Aaron puts his guard down.

"Can you talk with us a while out here?" Aaron suggests the lobby.

Dave agrees and frees himself of the kitchen area. Seeing the men take to a table, Dave seats himself with them. "What's this about?"

Aaron produces the old picture of Rebecca. "Is this Tanya? Tanya Kirkland," he adds while watching the man nod. Hearing the affirmation he continues, "And she is an employee here?"

"Was. This was her last day. She normally would still be here, except she has been having some migraines lately, so being the good guy I am, I let her go ahead and leave. You just missed her. You probably passed her coming in." Dave takes in their almost frenzied look. "What's this about?"

Trevor interjects with his own question, "Why is today her last day?"

Dave hesitates a second before answering. Seeing that they weren't going to even touch his question he offers, "Her husband was offered a better job. We'll miss her. She's been a great employee. Always on time, does her job, and I'll have a hard time finding someone to replace her."

"How long has she worked for you?" Trevor quizzes again.

"Just over a year-and-a-half." Dave states calmly. "Good person. So what is going on here? Is she okay?"

Trevor just smiles, "Yep. She's good. We're just checking on some things for her. We're old friends, and are disappointed we missed her today. We were in the area, you see?"

Dave could tell something isn't lining up, and flicked his gaze back and forth between the two men at the table. "Seriously, what the hell is going on?" He is starting to feel nervous.

Aaron tries a different approach. "She's part of an

investigation, and we want to make sure everything is going well with her and all that. Do you have any way to contact her? Her number?"

"Legally I can't give it to you," Dave says coldly. "Employee privacy and all."

"Could you call her?" Dave sits stone faced and flicks his eyes between them, so Aaron tries another way. "You mentioned this was her last day. Do you have any forwarding information for her?" Still Dave just sits, barely fidgeting under their direct looks.

"Does she hang out with any of her co-workers?" Trevor drills.

Dave stands up. "We're through here. I don't know what you two are up to, but Tanya has been a great employee who will be missed. You can't get anything else from me, or my crew. I must ask you to leave." His glare means business. "Now."

Trevor stands, and offers to shake Dave's hand, "Well, thanks for your time. We will be in touch."

Dave doesn't shake their hands. Nor does he move until he watches the car begin to pull out from his parking lot. As soon as it does, he takes the cell phone from his pocket and dials the number for Tanya. Chase answers the phone on the third ring. "Mitch, hi. It's Dave. I take it Tanya got home okay?" He listens. "Good, good. Hey, I just wanted to say...there were two guys in here just a second ago asking some weird questions about her. Do I have something I need to know?"

"Like what? I'm not sure I understand," Chase counters with.

Dave shrugs into the phone. "I'm not sure. They acted like those cops you see on TV, looking for a criminal. But I didn't tell them anything. I want you to know that." Dave hears a voice in the back ground of Tanya's line.

"Dave, thanks, but we're all good here. Maybe one of her brothers trying to cause trouble or something. Thanks for everything, but I have to go now. Talk to you later."

The line goes dead, and Dave is left wondering what is really going on.

CHAPTER 19

A freezing cold thought cuts me to the core, and I pull my jacket closer about my shivering body. Though I am sitting in Jay's small house, the biting end of Fall's edge touches me. My thoughts race as I sit there, knowing it wasn't said where we would go to at first. Mike thought we should go as far away from here as possible, and Chase agreed. I told them we weren't going to Alaska. They had looked at me like I was insane.

"Who said anything about Alaska?" Chase quipped in annoyance.

"Hawaii then?"

"What are you talking about?" He snapped again.

"Well," everyone was looking at me. "The way I see it, we are in the center of the US, when you fold it in half, and going south isn't going to be much better." Their eyes are still on mine. "What if we don't run that far? What if that helps us have roots, but don't leave too far away?"

Jay Strebeck is looking at me. Mike is looking at him. The kids are back to watching their movie. And Chase is glowering, at me of course. Who else?

Shaking my head slowly from side to side I continue with my thought. "Look. They found us. No one knows how." Chase mutters something about how he knows and that it's my fault and dumb dreams, so I speak over his mutterings. "They'd expect us to run far away from this place, wouldn't they?" Seeing Jay shrug and nod I continue, "So what if we just move to another town? One not so far away?"

Jay shakes his head and paces amongst us in the limited area or his living room. "No. I don't think that will help. Somehow they found you. Somehow they tracked you down. And somehow you started having dreams again." He takes in my look, and shakes his head. "No, somehow we need to find out what they did to track you down. We need to prevent those dreams if nothing else. We need to know what they know."

"What about your person on the inside," Mike chimes in.

Again a negative head shake. "That link is weak at best and not too privy to what we will need to know to stop this and make you all safe again."

Chase quips, "Aren't you worried for your own butts?"

Mike and Jay nod and share a quick glance before Jay continues, "We have lots of places to hide and go. We should be okay, but we need to be sure we aren't caught up with you Bec. That would be a serious hiccup to our lives and safety, not to mention yours."

Slowly I nod. A realization hits me like a lightning strike. "I cannot stay here." Seeing their confused faces, I offer more. "I cannot go to sleep here." My eyes find Chase's. "I am not dangerous. I didn't mean any of this. Please tell the kids I love them, and get them out of here safely." Full ramifications continue to hit me as I keep talking. "I doubt you'll ever let me see them or tell me where you are when you get settled, but...I don't think I have a choice here." He is still just looking at me. "I'll go." My eyes go around the room, thankful the kids are in another room. "I'll go."

The room is silent, and I look for my purse and pull out the divorce papers tucked within. Withdrawing a pen, I carefully open the documents and sign them. Replacing the pen I refold the legal paperwork and hand them to Chase without looking at his face. I head to the bedroom to grab some things.

No one moves.

No one follows me.

No one speaks.

This is what needs to be done. Once again, I have to be alone. Again, I have to seek a way to end this by myself. Part of me wonders if I will have the strength to be alone forever this time, to never see their faces again. Tears spring to my eyes and start dribbling down my checks as I look at their resting forms lost in the movie. My eyes memorize every line on their faces. Wiping my face on my sleeve I ensure they are tucked securely in, and back out of the room.

Without looking at the occupants of the living room, I reclaim my purse once again, and head to the door. No one moves yet. No one is speaking, but rather knowing this is the only way. I almost make it out the front door before anyone's voice breaks the silence of my departure.

"Bec, where are you going to go?" Not Chase's voice, but Mike's.

"Haven't a clue." And I walk out into the cold late fall night. My tears mingle with the cold rain on my shivering form as I take to the sidewalk, and pause. Wondering where I should go, I think a decent public hotel would be the best place to be picked up. Less spectacle and chance for personal harm. *Besides*, I convince myself, *a name brand hotel would offer more security and possibly a better night's rest.* My feet find motion on the wet pavement once again.

The long freezing walk in the rain here has given me an hour to form a plan, a test to see if they could track me, or if they got lucky with some other information leak giving our new found lives away. My plan was to stay at the hotel until I dreamt, which hopefully would be only a night or two, and see what the results were. If they could track me, then I guess they would find me, and I would have to deal with that. If not, maybe Chase would let me see my kids, like visitation or something. Either way, I had to have a safe harbor for the rest of the night, and my clothes were soaking wet.

    The sign at the lobby entrance still indicates rooms are available, so I enter. Walking up to the Front Desk, I pull out my fake identification of the last two years. "Do you have a single?" I never even looked up to see if it is a man or woman behind the desk, just had asked the question. So numb with worry, loss, and the cold, I follow the Front Desk worker's prompts, sign the credit slip for the room, and take the keycard. Solemnly I take to the stairs and head down the hallway towards my room for the night.

    Again, I wonder if they will be in the same hotel, or in the room next to mine, or above or below me. These two men who have come to look for me will have me right there, right in their sights. Panic hits me for what seems like the tenth time as I insert my keycard into my door's slot. The green light offers a small promise of "all clear" and I enter my temporary home and hit the light switch. Shrugging out of my water-logged jacket, I grope for a hanger to place it on. Taking in my surroundings I take off my soggy shoes and socks. Carefully I wring them out in the bathtub while the tears fill my eyes yet again. I continue until I am naked, and turn on the shower and the limited steam fills the small bathroom. My body heaves and nothing comes up. Fighting my upset, I finish my shower and look at the haggard person staring back from the mirror.

    My life is truly over.
Now if I can get some rest, some sleep.
That's not likely.
Fine, Tylenol PM it is.
You'll never dream with that in your system.
Fine, half a Tylenol PM it is.
Can't believe I have to talk to myself like this.
Can't believe I answer.

I shut up, take a half of a pill, and make my way to the bed.

CHAPTER 20

Breakthrough!
After days of trying, I feel like I have finally made the connection to join with my other. Taking a quick glance around, I realize she is in a dream. Nightmare would be more like it. The air is hot, stinky, like sweat and bad breath. I gag and fight back the urge to vomit. Looking around I don't see her. I don't see anyone. It's...scary. That's the only word I have for this feeling of absolute silence and terror that is mounting in my stomach as another round of nausea combats my senses. A loud bell tolls not too far above me, finally telling me I haven't lost my sense of hearing.
Something is definitely wrong here.
What I do see is an open field, or country, banked by hills before me. Behind me is a huge building, concrete or something, rising out of the ground like a modern castle. Its lack of windows leads me to wonder at how many levels this fifty foot wall really holds. I see two doors as the only lower level entrances on the wall, one not twenty feet away. The other steel door about a hundred or so feet away. A circular staircase made out of the similar concrete blocks looms above and beside me, another possible entrance to the complex.
Hearing the sound of terrified people running, I

turn. Coming at me are about twenty to twenty-five people. Quickly I scan the frantic faces for *her* face. She is running, pulling two young children along with her. She continues, looking over her shoulder, heading directly for me. No, to the compound behind me I realize as I can zero in on her thoughts.

Get them safe. Get them inside before they lock us out. I hear her thoughts as if they are my own.

I look over her shoulder at what causes this turmoil and terror within all the souls pounding towards me. Five small, dark moving shapes form from the air, getting larger with every passing moment. The breeze changes again, and the urge to hurl is growing as the shapes continue forming from the cloudy skies. The *whumpf, whumpf, whumpf* on the air is more discernible and getting closer. Instinctively, I know those objects materializing as if from the clouds are causing the sound, as well as the terror within all the people heading my way.

Please don't let the doors lock. We're almost there! Please wait for us. Please!

I look at my reflection only twenty feet from me. She briefly looks up, and then stumbles as she sees me.

"It's her," the boys calls. Hope resounds in his voice, so I offer a smile. I see her glance briefly at him as she pulls up next to me.

"You better run," she offers. The people are at the doors now, and then stop abruptly. They are pulling on the doors and pounding on the locked portals. They scream to those inside to open them for them. We both turn. "Oh no." Her voice sounds tired, like it has done this before and is not looking forward to the oncoming images.

I look my other half in the eyes. "What are we up against?"

She smiles a tired, half-hearted smile. "Dragons."
What? Dragons? What is going on here?

Her son takes my hand, and I am taken back by the surge of energy coming from him. "It's mommy's dream, but she didn't know we were going to check her dreams tonight."

It's the voice. *I know you, Little One.* Mommy's dream, huh?

Whumpf, whumpf, whumpf, whumpf....

"We don't have time for this. We have to get inside," she takes my hand, and the energy sparks between us. "We can still try going upstairs, but I don't like doing that. They can get you so easily that way." Some woman screams loud next to us. Her face a look of horror, and together we turn, seeing the five dragons of differing sizes are just above us. "Never mind. Get to the stairs, and follow my lead."

Whumpf, whumpf, whumpf, whumpf....

We take the few strides needed to put us by the circulating concrete spiral. Once there I notice what I hadn't had time to see before. A small space of a few feet separated the outside railing wall from the ceiling of the steps above us. Scorch marks mark the interior of the column holding the spiral in place, and instinctively I hug the outer railing and duck like the others before and after us.

Whumpf, whumpf, whumpf, whumpf....

Someone screams and gurgles, and then someone else screams in report. No doors open, nowhere for people to go. It's an attack with little protection. "Why aren't you protected? Why didn't they let you in?"

The son takes his hand from mine. "It's her dream, remember?"

The energy wants to take over, but I remind it to stay calm, tell it all is well. It doesn't listen, starts to move and counter the feelings around. More firmly I tell it to lie down, to listen to the idea of it being a realistic dream. The energy hovers, ready to do battle with mythical creatures of old. Chuckling, I turn to my reflective self, "You dream of dragons?"

Whumpf, whumpf, whumpf, whumpf....

She snorts her laugh out. "Yeah. Not really what I wanted to dream about. I can't get these two to go away."

Then she looks at me. "Can you help me?" The energy doesn't really come from me though, but from both of us, and the kids are wrapped into misty cocoons of living energy and whispered away. She looks at me in grateful response, but I knot my brow.

"I didn't do it all," I tell her. "It's from you too."

A snapping, hot, rancid mouth erupts through the slight crevice between the wall and ceiling near my head. The heat makes me duck and the urge to vomit chokes me. She puts up her hand, and the dragon snaps its head back in response. I had felt the energy rip around that head in an instant. Why did she think she had needed my help sending the kids away?

Whumpf, whumpf, whumpf, whumpf....

"They want to see what I can do in my dreams," she offers. "They think I am some sort of super hero or something." At my confused look, "Someone with special powers. I tell them only when I dream, and usually only with you."

Another scream from nearby draws my immediate attention. A man a few stairs down from me has a dragon head that has grappled his foot within its putrid teeth. My hand goes up...and nothing. The energy doesn't come for some reason. I try again, in vain as the man continues to freak out, trying to keep his hold the railing as the dragon tries to pull its catch from the stairwell. I look at her, and she slides down a few steps to see what is happening. Quickly she slides on her belly to the man. "Jimmy! Hold on!" Her face a picture of calm and rage at the same time, and she grabs his hand on the railing. With a quick flick of her wrist the boot the man is wearing slips from his foot, and the dragon makes off with its trophy.

Whumpf, whumpf, whumpf, whumpf....

He clings to her in gratitude for a brief second, before a scream above us draws her attention. Quickly we scramble up the stairs, keeping low and to the outer partition of the wall. As we near the screaming, we see two people smacking the nose of another larger dragon who is lifting its prey successfully out of the stairwell. And it is gone, and the screaming has stopped. Only tears and whimpers and spackles of blood remain on the staircase now.

The energy has had enough, has felt enough upset and pain. Again I tell it to rest, that this is only a nightmare, and again it won't listen to me. I hear it like a voice. It wonders why she won't stop them. She looks at me as if she has heard it, too.

Whump, whump, whump, whump....

Fire sizzles the air above our heads, and I think I am going to suffocate from the lack of breathable air during the onslaught. Though I know it's not real, I do feel the mounting panic building, and understand the energy's question. The intense heat continues for what I know is only a few seconds, yet it's like watching the scene in super slow motion. Seeing the lady just steps from me being scorched within those few seconds, no chance to repel the monster, and no time to scream in fear. Just charred alive, to a crisp, in a fraction of a second.

What a way to go.

She looks at me, her fear still on her face. Sorrow for a fallen friend hits her features for a fraction of time, then she swallows against the inferno. She stands, then charges down the stairs, and I have no choice but to follow. The energy starts to flow, nervous and timid, and not from me. She is in control in her dream, I begin to understand. She needs to do this, even though she doesn't really know she can.

So I tell her, "You need to stop this. This is all your making."

"The dreams don't stop. They continue, and live on like when I dream of your world. Every time I wake I don't remember everything though. But when I go back to sleep, I dream of being you...or this place." Her look is dismal. We are at the bottom of the stairs. "I only get so far. I can repel them for a few seconds, one at a time."

Whump, whump, whump, whump....

"Have you ever tried to take them all on?"

She looks at me like I am a moron. "At the same

time? That's suicide!"

I shake my head as I remind her this is a dream, that she is the one who is supposed to be in control. She looks terrified as she peeks at the base of the stairs, so I look. There was one dragon now, and I quietly remind her that this is her doing, and to take care of it.

"You!" she counters in a hissed whisper, and sidles up a few steps hoping it doesn't follow.

Too late...a gorgeous plume of flame is racing towards us as we continue back peddling up the stairs we just traversed down.

I see Two duck to the railing, still back peddling. She doesn't seem to share my fear about what is happening here. She doesn't really get it. I have been here dozens and dozens of times, and in all that time have been only able to bring the number of dragons down from seven to the five we have today. And that took a lot. The first many nights waking in tears and sweat, not really sure what I was reacting to or what the dream was. Finally I had convinced myself that this was the fear of being followed and hunted by the agency.

Her presence now told me that she is finally with me, something she hadn't been in two years. I flashback to only maybe fifteen minutes ago when I was running with Jay and Joanna and saw her standing there, taking everything in so calmly. Assessing, and scanning faces until she saw me. Relief had flooded me, as well as disbelief. Then Jay's words, like an answer to a prayer, "It's her." It had taken me aback. Now she's telling me to take control?

"You!"

She's backing up, not as afraid of the plume of fire that had just died down.

"There's five dragons out there!" I argue. But she isn't looking at me, she's turning away, towards the stairs going up. And I hear it, faintly, and my heart plummets.

"Mommy!"

"Jay!" Like I blur I fly up the stairs, skipping at least every other step, I almost leap, then taking two, or three. I can feel the energy pulsing through my veins, holding my heart in its protective grasp, gently squeezing and releasing it, helping me breathe though I am holding my breath in fear for my son's safety. The number of stairs I have passed are lost as I see the lightening of the staircase indicating my arrival at the top.

Whump, whump, whump, whump....

My son is there, and hovering a few feet above him is the largest one. I don't know where it came from, but it is hard to describe. All of a sudden I feel like my chest erupted and my soul wrapped itself around Jay. I feel the strong comforting hold of the energy hurl me in a controlled spin upwards like Mary Poppins. If the energy had been water I would be standing on a continuous gyrating geyser. When I was about even with the massive beast before me, I stop and hold myself right there, on the swirls of energy around me, and face it.

Whump, whump, whump, whump....

Another one is coming for me now too, a small female, and with a quick glance over my left shoulder made note of its position, and the energy remembers, alert. My body feels like it is hovering, like it could fly of its own accord with just a thought, like Superman.

The energy speaks, tells me my son is safe and to proceed.

Anger, and yet not anger, pours from me and those around me to give me strength, courage...power. It fills me, and I remember just over two years ago, and try to rein it in. *No massacres, just justice.* My breath comes in soft and slow, careful and measured, and mounting. Adrenaline courses through my veins, a friend of the energy running there. My companion and essence.

Time seems to stand still, and I can see every line on this dragon's massive, muscled body. And the awe of it fills me with a second of remorse. *No creature so beautiful should be condemned to die for no fault of its own. It is just trying to survive, too.*

Whump, whump, whump, whump....

The time has come I realize as a third, a young male, begins its descent on me, dropping sand into my little mental vortex of power. My eyes roll the slightest bit upward and see its wings descending rapidly, but not diving. Every dragon was within my grasp, and I can feel each of their hearts beating in its own time and rhythm with its own wings.

With regret and a touch of humaneness I place my right hand out in an effort of communication, "I am sorry."

The three don't grasp what I have said, but rather attack. With another swirl of energy, my geyser has my power whipping me quickly upwards to strike my hoverer with a force of a hundred dragons. Its form crumples mid-air and collapses from the force, and I toss his young form aside. Pain over what I had to do allows my left hand to hold the small female in mid attack by the neck. She twists and turns, hissing at the invisible hold I have on her. The massive male before me has risen up to where I am now and blown his fiery finest, but my tidal wave cocoon cools me and keeps me safe on my gyrating geyser of energy.

Again, "I am sorry."

He bellows his rage as I hold him, and reach to him, into his mind. Blind primal rage and animal hunger rule him, like I was a wolf smelling a wounded prey and wouldn't relent until one or both were dead.

"So sorry."

And he crumples right there, from a proud and magnificent creature to see, without fear telling you to run, to this bloody mass of broken bones, meat, and skin. Beautiful to grotesque.

The female howls in protest yet, but her mind now registers fear as she pierces me with her eyes. The others, hearing her howl have come to her aid. Somehow she has communicated her fear to them. I see it. Feel it. See them retreat to her side, trying to wrestle with an invisible beast. I feel their instincts of protection and what Darwin aptly named "fight or flight." Their urges spoke directly to me, and I understand.

"Don't come back." My hold releases her, and angrily she shakes herself to ensure she is no longer entrapped. A few flaps of her mighty wings, and she turns on her tail and literally heads for the hills. A total of three images fading into the cloudy sky, their cries and the sound of their wings dissipating rapidly with each powerful beat.

Gently the geyser slips from beneath me, lowering me to the top of the compound designed to protect us from the winged beasts departing. My son's quick arms wrap themselves around me before I remember he is there. His protective shell is still encasing him. With a mental flick, I waft it away.

Two walks up to me, a look of awe and congratulations on her face.

Jay looks up at me, "You really are a superhero Mom!

CHAPTER 20

RRRRIIIINNNNG!

    Aaron bolts upright in surprise while Trevor mutters a curse and gropes for a light on the nightstand by the bed. Trevor's hand finds a knob and light floods the area between their beds. Aaron's confused eyes focus on the alarm clock on the hotel's night stand. Reaching for the phone he grumbles about the time, "It's not even four thirty, for crying out loud!" Before Aaron can answer another earsplitting ring reverberates around the small room.

    Lifting the receiver, Aaron answers before it rings an irritating third time. He listens while confusion lights his face. "What?" He listens as Trevor searches is friend's face for information. "How long was the signal?...How long?" Aaron dart's another look at the clock. "Starting when?...And the second?...Really?"

    Trevor motions for information from his phone hog buddy, and is waved off.

    "A reconnect? Okay. Did we get a location?...That precise?...Well, yeah, I know that you had lots of time." His eyes roll. "Okay...gimme a second." Aaron motions for something to write with.

Trevor gets up and grabs Aaron's pen and notepad from the television stand and hands it over.

"Okay. Yes, I am ready....Are you sure?...Because that would be here...at the hotel!" Aaron looks at the room's door as if he can't wait to see what is on the other side.

Trevor's eyes light up even more and he starts pulling on some clothes knowing they won't be able to go back to sleep now. His gestures try to beg for more information from Aaron. Again he is waved off. "What!?" he finally blurts.

One lone finger is his answer.

Aaron's voice continues, "Yessir! We'll, get right on it....Right now, of course. We'll call you as soon as...yessir. Of course." He rolls his eyes, "Do you want me to continue wasting time listening to your threats and ideas or do you want Trevor and I to do our jobs?" He rolls his eyes, "Thank you." With that he replaces the receiver in the beige cradle and looks at his partner. "She's here."

"Got that much." Trevor finishes pulling on his attire. "I'm going to go down to the front desk and see what I can find out." With that he heads for the door, and hears Aaron's muttered curse and rummaging for clothes. "Be back in a jiffy."

No one was in the hallway as Trevor heads down to the front desk. A portly gentleman mans the desk as Trevor approaches. "Hi there. Friend a mine came in last night, maybe late. Didn' tell us she was gettin' in yet. Kirkland, Tanya Kirland. Could you tell me which room is hers?"

"Sorry. We can't give out that information. Security and all that." The man is taking in Trevor, so Trevor offers a look that spoke "Ah...shucks" something fierce. "But I could call the room for you."

Trevor then offers a tremendously grateful grin, "That would be great."

The front desk man smiles and looks back at Trevor while Trevor waits. "Uhm...now?"

Trevor nods, "That would be best. She won't mind."

Not altogether convinced the attendant asks again for the name of the party he's to call. "Once I reach the room, I will forward the call to that house phone." Trevor nods his understanding of actions about to take place.

Trevor hesitates for just a moment. He tries to watch what numbers the man was pushing, but the numbers were hit too quickly and the counter blocked a clear view. "Her husband, Mitch, might answer too. Make sure you talk to Tanya." Trevor backed away toward the phone in the lobby a few feet away, watching the front desk attendant.

"Who should I say is calling if she asks?"

Trevor offers a smile to his answer, "Chase." Watching the man from about twenty feet away he tries to eaves drop while he waited for the lobby phone to ring. He didn't expect it to so quickly. His hand shook for half a second before he answers. "Hello."

"That didn't take you guys long at all," came the sleep drugged voice.

"Well, it's taking us a lot longer than it should have," Trevor counters. "Can we end this now?"

"Depends. Do you know which room I am in?" Her voice is guarded.

Trevor decides to answer honestly. "No Rebecca, we don't. But we hope we don't have to get anyone else involved with this. It would be a shame to call the police and all that to watch the doors for an escapee. We could just be takin' you with us, no fuss, no fight, if ya let us." The line is quiet for a while, so Trevor thought he'd try more persuasion. "We'll let your family leave, of course. Just bring yourself down. You and the other one."

"'Other one?'" Her voice is really quiet now.

Trevor mentally kicks himself. "Anyone you think we might want to talk to or somethin'. We don't want problems, here, really. We just really want this to go as painless as possible for everyone. Just tell yer family you are stepping out, and they won't need to be privy to nothin' else." Trevor sees Aaron approaching and waves him over.

"You didn't answer my question," her voice is quiet,

yet calm. "Which...other...one?" Her tone leaves no room for negotiation.

"Tell you what. You meet me in the lobby, and you can tell us."

"Meet you in the lobby? Now?" Her voice lost control for a split second. "Either I meet you in the lobby, or you make a huge spectacle." Her control is now back in place. "Is that right?"

"Unfortunately," Trevor nods as he continues, "We'd prefer not to go that route, as I said earlier. So, just grab some of yer things and meet me and my buddy in the lobby. Public, no problems, no mess."

"Just the two of you? Not a dozen cars zooming around the corner?" Her voice displays all her contempt and uncertainty.

"I swear Rebecca. Just me and Aaron. My name is Trevor." He remains quiet for a moment to give her a chance to respond. When she doesn't, he offers a smile to his voice. "We can be real civil." Hearing her snort, he continues, knowing she is still there. "We, Aaron and I, have read your file. I know how Maxwell treated ya last time. Think we all learned our lesson last time, ta be honest." He motions to Aaron to be ready in case she bolts and they need to look for a running person. Aaron heads to the back hallway area, leaving Trevor asking, "So, what do you think?" No answer. "Rebecca?"

"Why did you say the 'other one'? Who are you talking about?" Again, a stern, controlled voice. She wasn't ready to give in without knowing every angle.

Trevor shakes his head, "Look, I shouldn't have said anythin'. Just another 'blip' as they call it shows up every so often lately, with you."

"Did it show up tonight?" Her voice was weak, nervous.

"Yes ma'am. It did." He notices her intake of breath. "Do you know who it is?" Silence greets him. "Rebecca?...Rebecca?"

The phone goes dead.

"Damn!" Trevor hisses, and reaches for his cell

phone. In an instant it dials Aaron's number. "She hung up on me. Keep an eye out fer her. I'll keep an eye out the front lobby way." Hearing his partner confirm, he hangs up. Pacing, he peers into the darkness of the world outside. His thoughts have him second guessing every shadow and light flickering he sees.

So intent on his watch he didn't see her reflection as she approaches from behind him. "You said you had a partner?" Trevor spins around to face her, ready for a fight or her flight. Her stance is wary, but her eyes meet his. "You also said you were civil. Or, was that a lie too?"

"I don't lie, ma'am," Trevor assures. "Trevor."

"Where's your partner?" Her eyes don't leave his.

"You see, we were afraid you'd try to flee or somethin'."

"You better get him in here then, don't you think, as I am not running." Her face is a mask, her voice short and controlled.

Trevor looks her over, and sees her sleep-roughened state. "You look different than your picture." With that he pulls out his phone and hits redial and waits for it to be answered. When it is, "She's in the lobby with me," then flips it shut. "Your family know your goin'?" She only nods in kind. "Are they gonna flee without ya?'" Nothing, not even a blink or wince. "They takin' off, that why you don't want him out back?"

"You said my family could leave." Again that steady stare and controlled tone.

"Sure they can. We would like the other one though." She doesn't move. "It would help if we could take both of you into custody at-"

"Custody?" Concern, alarm fills her voice.

Placing his hands before himself, Trevor tries to placate her. "Just a term we use, I swear. What would you rather it be called?"

She never breaks his gaze. "I don't know who else you could be talking about. I heard that my other, my dream alter ego if you will, was always traceable before. Perhaps that is what you're reading?"

Trevor sees Aaron quickly approaching, and places himself between Aaron and Rebecca for introductions. He also fills Aaron in that he had assures her that her family can leave and wants Aaron to back his claim up. Aaron does, and she seems satisfied. "The agency is mostly interested in you, in your readings and hence your abilities," Aaron continues. Aaron listens as Trevor conveys Rebecca's thought of the other signal being from her other dream world self with Rebecca filling in limited pieces of information. Realizing they are still all standing, Aaron offers they sit on the sofas in the lobby.

As Rebecca reluctantly agrees, they offer quick glances to each other thinking her family was sneaking out into the darkness with her technique. But they resume talking briefly as to her theory, and how she would like to go back to the agency.

"To be honest, I wouldn't like to go back at all," is her reply. When prompted for a reason, "The energy, the atmosphere, there was negative...painful."

Aaron smiles and reaches to touch her hand gripping the armrest of the sofa. Her flinch tells him his touch isn't welcome nor appreciated. "Not all of us are Maxwells in the agency." Her look tells him she doesn't believe that at all, but he shrugs it off. "You see, we have a job to do here. We are *required* to bring you back. We *need* you to come back. We need your help."

"My help?" she snorts.

"All those people who are under the agency's protection, some of them willingly, mind you, need your help." Aaron saw the quick glimpse of pain and regret before her guarded façade reclaims her features. "You didn't know, did you?"

Her blank look answers his question.

"You didn't kill the other experi-, the others, like you." Her mouth parts a bit, so Aaron presses forward. "Every single one of the others was either comatose, or...without their ability. Some still are."

Her blank look continues.

Trevor tries, "Do you like your...ability?"

She looks down into her lap for the first time. Her stillness throws them a moment. When Rebecca finally speaks, they have to listen carefully as she is so quiet. "I didn't know I had an *ability* until my whole life was ripped away from me, my family, my friends, my home, my history." She looks into their faces. "All for what? Some dreams I have?" She meets their looks, and continues. "I didn't know anything about an *ability* until the agency said I had one and wanted to tear apart my world, and that of my family." Her eyes hit them accusingly now. "And just so you know. It did. My...family is...a mess because of you guys." She shakes her head again. "If dreaming is an 'ability', I'd rather not dream than have gone through what I have had to."

Trevor and Aaron look at the brunette before them with new understanding. Long moments of silence impregnate the air of the lobby. No one speaks nor moves for about three minutes. It is only broken by the ring of the front desk phone. Trevor and Aaron look at Rebecca, who slowly stands and glances between them.
"Are we going now, or can I get some stuff from my room to take along?" Seeing their worried faces, she adds. "Of course, you can follow me to my room."

And Trevor does.

Aaron excuses himself to make the call to Roberts as they leave. "She's coming with us. No fight, no fuss."

"Good."

CHAPTER 22

    The view of the terrain we pass holds little interest for me. Gone is the late fall look of Wisconsin. I realize how much I will miss the pristine snow in Wisconsin's winter, and the lush vivid greens and warmth in the summer. No longer would I have the white Christmas, be able to pick out my tree from a local tree farm. No longer would "local grown" Jennie-O turkeys grace my table. Now they'd have to be trucked in from someplace else, but then again, I won't be buying them anymore, now would I?
    This is the day after the lobby incident, and I am back with the agency. Trevor and Aaron are driving me back, to New Mexico, and I was dreading what would be waiting for me there. These two keep telling me that some of the "experimentals" or "others" didn't mind being there within the compound. For some, if I was to believe Trevor and Aaron, actually felt at home within the agency's grip. Some had been invaluable to research and national security or something of that nature.
    Their friendly talkative nature didn't set me at ease, nor did I wish to participate in their question asking. In fact, more than once I had asked them to end the interrogation and silence would fill the car until the next "pit stop." So here I sit in the back seat of their rented

vehicle traversing through Oklahoma thinking of, no, dreading, what lay before me, and my future lack of family and love.

With a deep sigh, I remember when Trevor "escorted" me back to my hotel room. Thankfully he waited outside while I drafted a quick note to Chase and Jay, in code, just in case, saying who I was with and that I hoped they would be as safe as I was promised. I also penned that I knew for certain all the others hadn't been killed as we had thought, but were safe, and hoped that would ease the anger in Chase's heart towards me. Using the room's phone, I had called Chase's cell phone number. I didn't really expect him to answer, but hearing his voice requesting the caller to leave a message had been both disturbing and comforting. My message to him had been brief and instructed him to pick up a package at the hotel's front desk in his current name.

When I emerged from the room, Trevor offered to help carry my limited supply of belongings. With a determined shake of my head, I had told him I wanted to leave some things at the front desk. No question then, just his presence back to where we had met.

Then Aaron pulled up to the front doors, and we left. They kept checking in with someone, who must have been the very anal Roberts, for it was almost every hour he called, except when we had stopped in a hotel last night and Aaron had called him to tell the man they needed rest and to wait until they called him in the morning to report any updates. The reprieve from the incessant ringing was nice, but I still hadn't been able to sleep. We had to get the suite that had the bedroom nearest the door. I was in the smaller room to the back with no windows, the prisoner.

Now, like a convict of some heinous crime, I am being "bussed" to my new prison. Trevor had assured me a nice, private room would be waiting for me. In addition, I was promised a private bathroom and television if I continued to offer no resistance or tried to flee.

"To where?" had been my retort. "You'd find me as soon as I fell asleep." My constant derogatory comments were wearing on them, I knew, but I wanted them to see what it was like from my angle. It sucked, plain and simple. I won't try to sugar coat it.

My spirits had been lifted every time my captors spoke of the survivors, and though I didn't pry for information, they told me lots. I learned some about who the survivors were, and that Aaron and Trevor had actually brought three of them to the agency over the past several years. Two of them had remained in "friendly" contact with my current captors if Aaron was to be believed. They were siblings, twins, actually, from what I gathered, but with little real power or ability. They somehow tripped the agency's "somebody" sensor, and could remember things very, very well, but that was about the general extent of the usefulness of Caleb and Corrine Casten. Apparently the Casten siblings had been with the agency for eleven years, and were the ones who helped rebuild the files that had been wiped by the devastation of two years ago. In a sense, they worked for the agency. It was commented on that recently they couldn't remember nearly as much as they used to, nor were they able to retain any current information with clarity. I was made to feel I was the reason for their...inabilities.

The third person Aaron and Trevor had brought had some abilities of interpretation of water and weather, the movement and density, weird stuff. In Trevor's southern slang, he made it sound like this Nigel had been having a really bad week with work and a soon to be ex-wife taking him for everything and he accidentally caused Hurricane Katrina. Trevor joked that if Nigel woke up, the two of us might actually get along. Aaron had mentioned that maybe it would be safer if Nigel stayed comatose, and I wondered if he feared Nigel, or if he was trying to make a joke.

During our travel I had heard about a Sam. From their discussion I never heard if it was a man or a woman, but it was indicated that he or she was an older experimental who could empathize emotions and sometimes visualize images those that Sam touched. Apparently this Sam was awake and trying to wake the others to no avail.

An older male named Dale had been used in international government treaty meetings and hostage release situations. His ability to negotiate and read minds had been extremely valuable, so the government was more than a little anxious to see if he could read mine. Trevor had chimed in, "Think of a gran'parent givin' ya a touch on the cheek or somethin', and bringin' a smile to yer face. Yep, you'd definitely like Dale."

Genevieve was by far the oldest case they had, and had been with the agency an impressive thirty some years. Her ability was also coded as energy, though it was hinted she didn't have nearly the ability that it was speculated I had. Apparently she had been asking to meet with me prior to...that day.

Robert and Bob were both time-benders...or something. I didn't fully understand, but since I was being difficult and not asking questions, I guess if I ever met either of the two I would have to find out for myself. Apparently, they had no memory of what they were capable of since...yes, that day.

I was starting to feel guilty for what I had allowed to happen to these people. But it wasn't like I had chosen this kind of thing to happen, nor did I want to hurt them. It had been the energy's choice. *But doesn't that make me an accomplice?*

Then the faintest of whispers announces her presence. *Now is not a good time*, I warn.

Why? What's going on? She's guarded.

I'm back with the agency.

What? I hear the panic in her thought and see the images flash across our link.

I turned myself in. To save my family. Quickly I mentally summarize all that has transpired, and where I was, and what I now know. Also, I include what I know of the survivors, and how everyone was hoping by bringing me back they'd also get back their experimentals. Only silence answers me. *Are you still there?*

Yeah. Just astonished is all. So what's the plan?

Plan?

Yeah, are you going back to tear the place up again and free the others, or what?

Nope. I'm just going. I have nothing else to look forward to now.

For a long time I ride in silence. Aaron's phone rings, about twenty minutes early. After Aaron answers, he turns and looks at me. "Yes. She's right here....I am looking at her." He rolls his eyes. "Okay, I'll ask." He addresses me fully, pulling the phone from his ear. "Are you alone?" he asks in a mock acting voice he must be mimicking from some class B movie.

"No," my eyes lock with his.

His eyes bore into mine for a second, and I can hear the frantic Roberts piping up to have Aaron's ear once again. Again Aaron's eyes find mine. "Sir, I don't think that an armed escort will be helpful, nor necessary."

I don't blink, smile, frown, nor speak. *Think what you will.*

Aaron's eyes blink. "Holy crap!" Trevor and Roberts are both asking what in panicked tones, but Aaron's eyes are on me. "Did you...you...just?"

What? I can feel the energy now, and I understand what his look and mannerisms are about.

Aaron gives me a hard look, then tells the two who are still asking what's happening that he thinks he just read my mind or something.

Two laughs, *Is this guy for real?*

"*She just did it again!*" Aaron squawks. Then he listens intently on the phone while watching me. "She's not moving her lips, Sir." Again he listens, "Yeah. About two more hours or so....Okay....Okay." After receiving a few more instructions, he hangs up and gives me a weird look.

Trevor glances nervously at his partner. "What the heck is goin' on Aaron?"

Aaron locks eyes with mine once again. "I think I just got a touch of her ability."

Two snorts, *Touch? I think he was touched to begin*

with.

I cannot help but smirk at her joke, and his shocked face. He scowls and faces forward. Regardless, he starts his interpretation of what just transpired for Trevor. Two doesn't like his story, so decides to tell Trevor herself.

Poor Trevor.

Please don't do that again. He's driving. He could've just killed us all, I tease. Finally I have someone I want to talk with. And her sense of humor is just what I need.

CHAPTER 23

I remember meeting with people when I arrived at the compound. The names elude me some, okay...mostly. Roberts I remember. Briefly. Yet, the presence of one like that leaves an impression.

I can still smell the fresh paint, new grout, and the stale scent of new metal. The energy of those of before lingered, too. There had been the others. I could feel them, their energy.

"Two." My lips crack upon saying it for what seems like the millionth time today.

Weird. I don't remember how many days it has been.

"Two." My voice comes out in a warble. It sounds foreign, even to me.

The food comes and goes. The drinks, too. Sleep is always present. But not the dreams. Not the every day. At first I wanted to think I was depressed, but I feel asleep during that thought process.

Somehow I have little idea, little presence. That frightens me.

"Two. Help me." My voice is a hoarse whisper caked in despair.

No visits. No memories. No life.

I am being drugged. Kept asleep. Kept immobile

and inactive.
    I feel the sleep coming on, and I can no longer fight it. I need help.
    Two!

Bureau of Federal Energy and Interest   NRG-ASE

Case #: R00013ASE   Case Name: Rebecca
DOB: 07/23/1974   Code: energy

CLASSIFIED

Observation time/date: 09 November 2008/1733hrs
Report type: Weekly follow-up
Time in observation: 23 days
Weight: 160lbs
Status: continued drugged/sedation, still no signals while sedated
Method of medication: airborne

Notes:

Rebecca (Case #: R00013ASE) continues to be sedated per Robert's orders. Initial doses of sedative prevented proper nutrition as subject refused to eat or drink after sedative worked. Subject has lost over 9 pounds since arriving, also continues to exhibit loss of motor skills.

Review of tapes continues to show despondent behavior. Only word spoken since shown her quarters continues to be "to." This word is spoken every few minutes, or less. No measurable or discernable pattern when speaking "to.' Still no dialog with contacts or physicians when present in subject quarters.

New transmitter chip surgically installed with success.

Physicians are concerned with subject's apparent depression and are lowering the dose of sedative in miniscule proportions to ensure safety of subject and compound as a whole. Sedative will be introduced back into subject's diet as soon as possible.

Bureau of Federal Energy and Interest

DD Form 99-ASE   BFEI-USA   Subject Record

Bureau of Federal Energy and Interest   NRG-ASE

Case #: R00013ASE   Case Name: Rebecca
DOB: 07/23/1974   Code: energy

CLASSIFIED

Observation time/date: 16 November 2008/1703hrs
Report type: Weekly follow-up
Time in observation: 30 days
Weight: 158lbs
Status: continued drugged/sedation
Method of medication: airborne and dietary additions

Notes:

Rebecca (Case #: R00013ASE) continues to be sedated per Robert's orders. Initial doses of sedative prevented proper nutrition as subject refused to eat or drink after sedative worked. Subject has lost over 11 pounds since arriving, and motor skills have deteriorated.

A minute energy has been detected from the subject, but only twice, and while subject was sedated. Subject denies (headshake only form of indication) any knowledge, but for a moment looked "hopeful."

Review of tapes continues to show despondent behavior. Only word spoken since shown her quarters continues to be "to." This word is spoken every few minutes, or less. Still no measurable or discernable pattern when speaking "to." Still no dialog with contacts or physicians when present in subject quarters. Robert's authorizes mass force and aerial assault of sedatives as necessary.

Bureau of Federal Energy and Interest

DD Form 99-ASE   BFEI-USA   Subject Record

Bureau of Federal Energy and Interest   NRG-ASE

Case #: R00013ASE   Case Name: Rebecca
DOB: 07/23/1974   Code: energy

CLASSIFIED

Observation time/date: 28 November 2008/1640hrs
Report type: Weekly follow-up
Time in observation: 42 days
Weight: 154lbs
Status: sedated
Method of medication: airborne

Notes:

Rebecca (Case #: R00013ASE) continues to be sedated. Energy sikes are noted with this as well.

Atrophy has definitely been noted. Chris will work more on this issue to see what can be done.

Bureau of Federal Energy and Interest

DD Form 99-ASE   BFEI-USA   Subject Record

Jodie M. Swanson

CHAPTER 24

Like a siren's wail, I heard her. Weak, hurt, haunting. She called for me. One lone word. Her nickname for me. *Two.* I had waited for her by the water, waited watching the waves touch my toes, and waited some more. But no more came from her. She called because she needed me. Problem was, I didn't know where to find her. Where they took her, those government people she had hid from, I wasn't sure. She had been positive it was the same place as before, I remember feeling that when we were in the car with those two men. She had asked me to go, to leave her in peace so she could do and be. I hadn't understood, not fully.

Sure, I knew her sense of life and purpose had deteriorated with Chase's betrayal. I also understood her need to try and make sense of this without me in her mind, using her energy. I knew she had done what she felt she needed to try to make things right and end her life on the run as she had called it. But, not having me be with her when she went back there. That I didn't really get. I knew how she felt about that place, and was definitely stronger than her. Before she was afraid they'd break her. That she'd...

That was it. She had been ready to die. To let the agency experiment on her and break her down, kill her if they must. A cold shiver slithers around me in the energy's frustration.

But she called me. She needed me. Needs me.

That was a good sign. But I wasn't sure how to find her. It had been over two months since they had taken her to that place, the agency she had called it. I had sought her out many times, but to no avail. I needed another piece, another call for help.

"Excuse me?" a soft voice says drawing my gaze. He is a young man, blonde and boyishly handsome.

"Yes?"

Are you the one who helped my mommy?

I stand still, stare really. This boy's lips didn't move. His eyes bore into mine.

Are you the one who helped my mommy?

I don't breathe.

"Never mind," he says as he turns and starts to walk away.

The sentence had hung so strong in the air, so powerful and simple, but the memory hit stronger. It was the voice from so long ago. From a dream that had awaken me and left me paralyzed, left me in a dreamland stupor. And the person belonging to the voice was here, as clear as day. My eyes watch his back as he continues to walk, then joins hands with a young lady of similar coloring and stature. The blonde girl's eyes had been on me I realize.

Come on, the boy says to her. *I guess I was wrong.*

Her eyes are still on me, and I can hear her answer him. *But we were so sure. Now what do we do?* She has finally taken her eyes from me and meets his instead.

We keep looking. Mom never gave up. She always gave herself up for us. Every nightmare. Every time they came for her, she protected us. Now she needs us. He watches her bob her head in agreement. *Come on. Let's keep looking.*

I can no longer stand it. The energy won't let me. It has started screaming in my ear. My fear still touches me, but the energy is taking over. My hand goes up and the word comes from my mind loud and clear as if I had called across the distance. *Wait!* Slowly the two blondes look at me, wary. The energy lifts me and I glide toward them.

The boy shields his sister with his own scrawny being.

Gently I hover beside them, *Who are you?* My feet rest just above the sand.

The boy thinks, and I can see and almost read what he tries to work out to say. "Help me," and then the tears fall in earnest. He knows who I am, and I can only guess who these talented energy special children are. "Please," he continues. "She can't dream. They won't let her."

The girl steps from behind her sibling. *Please help us. We just want to know if she's okay.*

The energy gently sets me down now. "How can I refuse such gifted children," I hear the words I think tumble from my lips. I smile seeing their hopeful ones touch their teary faces. "But come, let us go somewhere we can talk more freely." With that I walk, leading them towards my small home. They follow wordlessly, quickly, and I know their urgency is in every movement.

Once there I ask them what they know. Interesting is that they know their mom did sacrifice her life with them to protect them from all this hurt and constant running from the agency seeking them. They seem to know a lot. They talk a lot. But not much about themselves, or how they found me. Before and now. Carefully I tell him what he had done to me all those months ago, and that something like that had never happened to someone like me before. The boy cringes when I mention "before," like one who has been caught doing something wrong and is about to be punished. Again, I feel the energy assure me to make things right, and I do what I am told.

For what seems like hours we talk about what they know, how they had to adapt and change their identities to protect their mother, and then comes the question from him. "She hasn't dreamed since she left. I can't find her when I am sleeping. Usually when I am in trouble she finds me and makes everything better. Lately, she's not there. Can you help?"

We talk about these past dreams some more, and decide to "see" what they really can do. I ask the energy, and it moves, softly, carefully, like a caress across every strand of hair on their heads, and I can tell they know this feeling. The girl softly calls for her mom, and I see them succumbing to a quick, yet gentle, sleep. Seeing the uncomfortable angle of their drooped heads, I shift their sleeping forms until they lay on their backs in a prone position. Then the energy comes to me. I remember the dragons and seeing the son there, and her vicious protective display, and I know what how to find her.

Forgive me, my friend.

Carefully into the sleeping innocents before me, I insert the world of *her* nightmares. A very good replica of what I remember, a fortress of sorts. Stairs charred from past encounters, and I see him reach for her, and across the space between them their hands clasp, but never touch. I see her face him, eyes closed, and him almost expectant. His soft voice hisses, "Get ready. This is the one I told you about."

Insert me.

They see me and break into a run to me. I put my hands up, and they stop. "I'm not your mom. She calls me '*Two.*' Or you can call me Bec." They drop their shoulders in their upset. I catch their eyes, making sure I have their attention. Then I look at the boy. "Are you sure you want to do this? This is her world, her nightmare. I don't know how to fight her dragons."

The girl, still holding her brother's hand, steps behind her sibling. "Are there really dragons?"

I reach out, looking for any tendril of her presence. Time seems to stand still as I keep searching, feeling, waiting. Seconds pass, then minutes. People pass us and greet me as if I am her. I smile and nod, not daring to speak, not wanting to betray her and her friendships with these people. Some people look at the children, and I realize this isn't right. The people don't understand who these kids are with "me." And so I take a hold of the boy's free right hand. "Come on."

We begin walking toward the scorched desert skirted with limited trees, and rim of mountains, away from her secure fortress. People haven't paid us much mind, and we quickly move away from them, and their civilization. We walked for almost a mile straight towards where I had seen my first dragons.

Then, like a distant candle, a whimper.

The kids exchange excited glances.

Insert dragons.

The grip on my left hand tightens tenfold and I look into the boy's face. "Don't worry. She'll come." Carefully, I head toward the nearest trees with my precious cargo in tow. I reach out again. *Come on.*

The girl's voice whispers, "We heard that."

Carefully I place my forefinger across my lips indicating a sudden need for silence. I am listening. For dragons. And for her.

Whumpf.

Still faint. But yet again the grip on my left hand increases.

Whumpf.

Come on, Rebecca. Where are you? My senses strain for any sign of her presence.

Whump-whumpf. Whumpf.

The girl whimpers and her brother shushes her behind me. My eyes are peeling the terrain looking for my double.

Whumpf, whump-whumpf.

"There's three of them," he whispers beside me.

Again a solitary finger to indicate silence. My eyes still don't see her, but my ears pick up on the terrified screams and obvious panic from the fortress as the settlers there rush to safety.

Whumpf. Whumpf.

My eyes flit to the dark forms becoming more and more defined with every thrust of their leathery wings. Definitely three, two large and a smaller, are coming. *I was kinda hoping we'd only have to deal with one.*

Me too.

He is so cute. *Don't worry. She'll come. But...the dragons aren't attacking us.*

I go dumb for a second. *He's right.* And dumb again. Slowly, I turn to see their hands still clasped, and nervous faces. And they are here to put themselves in danger to see their mom again. *Are you sure about this?* She looks to him for strength, and he nods at me. He lets go of my hand. And before I know to grab him back, they are running for the fortress, knowing they will never make it. My mouth drops.

Damn.

Bureau of Federal Energy and Interest   NRG-ASE

Case #: R00013ASE   Case Name: Rebecca
DOB: 07/23/1974   Code: energy

CLASSIFIED

Observation time/date: 4 December 2008/1617hrs
Report type: Weekly follow-up
Time in observation: 48 days
Weight: 144lbs
Status: semi-alert
Method of medication: NA

Notes:

Rebecca (Case #: R00013ASE) was removed from sedation per Roberts' orders. Subject has lessened motor skills, atrophy, and vomited.

Energy levels from the subject have been detected since subject has been revived.

Review of tapes continues to show despondent behavior. Only word spoken since shown to her quarters is "to". Limited dialog with contact, but not with physicians or Roberts, when present in subject's quarters. Chris has volunteered to assist as necessary.

Bureau of Federal Energy and Interest

DD Form 99-ASE   BFEI-USA   Subject Record

Jodie M. Swanson

CHAPTER 25

Like a siren's wail, I hear her.
Damn.
Déjà vu. Feel something so strong. Pulls me. A strong sense of panic.

It's like opening my eyes for the first time. I whirl around, trying to get my bearings. The light burns my eyes. And there's heat. No, fire. It's fire.

Am I on fire?

Blinking. It hurts. Everything hurts, like I haven't moved in days, weeks. My eyes start to focus.

I know this place. The terrain, yes, the mountains in the distance, the trees sporadic and a vast desert type plain. *I do know this place...oh crap! Oh my God!* I definitely know the two blonde kids hurtling themselves towards me, hands clasped, running as thought their lives depended on it. *Now why would that...oh crap and hell!*

Whumpf! Whumpf, whumpf!

"*NO!*" For a second they didn't see me, too terrified and rightfully so. They keep glancing over their shoulders. "Don't look back! This way!" I realize I am already running towards them. Well, stumbling would be more accurate. My steps are uncoordinated, like I've definitely had way too much to drink. "Help me," I plea the energy I can almost feel buzzing next to me. It feels foreign. "Please help me." I fall to the ground.

Trying to get up, I see Jay and Joanna continue to peer over their shoulders as they run, and now I see her. Two is running, but her eyes are on me, not the three incoming dragons. She seems to be flying, and soon I realize she really is. She overtakes my kids and scoops their forms and swirls towards me like something out of a Sci-Fi movie. She lands next to me and the three of them collapse on me. I am reminded of a Mommy Pile moment long past.

"Okay, okay you two. Let her up," Two chides as my kids detangle themselves from me.

Struggling to stand, knowing the danger coming, I look to say something, but cannot. So I just reach out to her, "I can't...please help."

She just smiles. *It's okay. Look. Seriously, look around.*

Gentle swells greet my weary gaze. I should have known she wouldn't let us get hurt, that she'd take us from harm. *Damn, she's good.*

I know. Her smile never falters. But her eyes dart to the blondes standing in the sand next to her. *Good, talented kids you have here.*

Anger contorts my emotions in a second. *How dare you put them in that place! That dangerous situation! What were you thinking?*

Their idea, she snips back.

At once my munchkins start recounting their plan and the execution of it while I continue to kneel in the sand. After a few minutes, I give up any hope of standing and sit instead, allowing their tale to continue. I listen as they talk about telling Two what they can do, "dream-link" Two had called it, and Two's plan of trying to exploit my motherly need to protect them. Jay piped up how he realized that he and Joanna weren't in danger, and that is why they left my double, to put out the vibes that they really needed me. Two added that she thought of the place knowing it was my nightmare place, where I had control and lots of power, hoping it would help.

But after a bit, I was so exhausted. My eyes felt tired, and though I was sitting, I felt I was falling down. Two's concerned face told me she could see it, and told my kids to go, that she would help me, but they needed to leave now, and they could come back another time soon. When they fought that, Two sent the energy after them, and they were gone. My last glimpse of them.

She kneels beside me, placing an arm around me.

"I'm so tired," I whisper. Reminds me of counting down with an anesthesiologist before going under the knife. "What's...wr-wrong with...m-me?" Every fiber in my body is both falling asleep and fighting to stay awake.

Two holds my hand. "It's okay. I've got you. I've got you now."

My eyes grow too heavy, and the world is a void once again.

"Holy Toledo! Did you see the spikes on Rebecca's chart? Unbelievable!" Johnston was still chirping away as Roberts looked over the computer screen and the readings there. "She just lit up like...like...like Edward does when he's not under. Dang!"

Roberts shakes his head at her misplaced enthusiasm, but he had to admit, he was glad he actually got to witness it firsthand. He had just come by to check on her status as they had almost fully eliminated her airborne sedative piping into her quarters. She hadn't eaten in days, but had only been awake a total of just over five hours each of those days. The physicians had asked him to come and let them check her over, that they were concerned for her wellbeing. Obviously, she wasn't as weak as they thought her to be, despite her continued weight loss and apparent loss of motor skills. She seemed to fire on all cylinders on the monitors and scales in place.

"Can you let go of the button now, Sir?" Johnston asks carefully.

Roberts looks to see he is still pressing the panic sedation button that had flooded Rebecca's room full of sedative and effectively ended her little episode. He let go and resumes looking at the continued stream of information still compiling and waits. While he does, he again peers through the safety glass at the woman sleeping on the mat. She was a complex case, and Johnston had it right in one sense. Rebecca had definitely lit up the screen like Edward, their most dangerous and hostile subject.

Edward was the very meaning of terrorist, and why Roberts still had a job. Luckily, Edward was one of the subjects who was comatose, and in a sadistic sense, he was grateful for Rebecca's last compound visit. Actually, for two reasons: all the upgrades to all their technologies, and of course, having an unconscious and incapable Edward. No more F5 tornados, Category 5 hurricanes, just to play a power trip. No taking control of airplanes filled with innocent people just to push a point. Edward was why Roberts was afraid of Rebecca. If she could and would do any of what Edward can and did, they'd have to keep her as docile and comatose as Edward currently was.

Roberts looks back at the information graphing itself appropriately on the screen, and gasps. "Johnston? Are there any other subjects in this wing that are awake?"

"No, Sir. Why?"

"We have multiple energy signatures being read here."

"What?" Johnston joins Roberts in front of the screen. "That's not right. Is it?"

Roberts ponders it a second. "Well, we did have a faint second signal prior to her acquisition, correct?" Hearing the affirmation he knew would come, "Well, then three isn't too far out of the question?" Seeing his assistant shrug in shock, he taps the monitor. "Maybe we do need to sober her up and start seeking her help on this. We need to find out why in her file from years ago she had two signatures and why they had labeled some 'full recall.' I think I am missing something here." He looked back at the sleeping Rebecca. "In fact, I think I am missing someone here."

CHAPTER 26

"As far as we know, it is like...like...a computer sending and receiving. She transmits and receives. We can read the waves she sends and receives."

Roberts looks at the man before him. "I know that. What I want to know is how we know she has full recognition? And that there is this other 'self' or whatever? How do we even know about that? I have been in charge of these cases and persons, but most don't link like Rebecca does. Why is that? Who is, and what is, the other transmitting and receiving? Who is it, and how the hell do they do it?"

"We don't know, and have no way of knowing. The signal isn't from our territories. We cannot triangulate," seeing Roberts brows raise, "Get a fix?"

"Damn it, I know what triangulate means! What I don't understand is *why*? You have all this technology, satellites and antenna units reading the entire Earth, and you cannot triangulate? How is that possible?"

The man frowns as he taps the keyboard before him. "It's like...okay. You know we can read some of the other countries' persons of interest, right?" A nod answers him. "It is like tracing something that isn't. Those other countries don't even have one like Rebecca. She is unique. She and that other one she links up with. It's like an invisible...no, more like another dimension or-"

"If you are going to say 'from another planet', I am going to vomit."

"Look, you ask how it's possible. No one knows, and until two years ago, and she actually sustained communication with this other entity or whatever, no one truly cared."

Roberts' face offers no compassion. "We all cared when she destroyed what we built."

The man raises his eyebrows. "Makes you wonder why she destroyed it."

Roberts turns to leave, "And how."

This visit with the analytical programmer had been truly and utterly disappointing. With Edward they had known what was happening, and from where, and how to control it. He couldn't do the "link" thing like Rebecca could, or at least he didn't appeared to. Nope, Edward was a different case altogether.

There are many movies and books out there speaking to the heightened cranial activity mixed with uncontrolled raging hormones triggering the reaction in many of the compound's inmates. No one knows for certain why or how, but the brain just does. Some of the things the brain can make a human body do. It can make someone lift heavy objects. Hold their breath past believing thresholds. It can forget what it wants, and learn exponentially. It helps people believe they can commune with the dead. And, of course, it can be the most unpredictable weapon unless harnessed properly.

Edward's signals started in his teens, with the onset of puberty, like most it seems. His first kiss ended with a rogue F1 tornado ripping through the neighborhood, sparing his home, and killing a mere two people in his small town of nearly two thousand. Edward continued to emit signals, powerful ones, and every time something momentous happened in his life, so did something disastrous. An instance during Basic Training for the military really threw California into a series of earthquakes with varying ranges on the Richter scale. Another with a broken heart caused the devastating Hurricane affecting Homestead AFB, Florida, a few years later. But being the military already had their hands on him, Edward never really saw all the specialized experimentation he was being subjected to as anything above and beyond what duty called for. He never questioned because he had been trained not to. He was like most GIs, a mushroom, fed crap and kept in the dark.

Within his first few days at the compound, and he had known something was amiss. "This place is wrong. What am I doing here?" he had asked Roberts that day.

"We need you. You have some...abilities, training, we need here," Roberts had said as he had indicated for Edward to take a seat.

"What training?" The air had seemed to change from military bearing to prison in that instant. Edward had felt it, and all hope to have this asset had changed to liability. Instead of channeling his energy towards our nation's security, it had put the nation at risk. Sessions became taxing on the counselors and Edward learned about what he was capable of via the series of questions, having never put the pieces together on his own before. He threatened exposure and escape, and became hostile.

Roberts recalled the day Edward's re-enlistment day came, and Edward refused to sign. They had pleaded for him to sign the paperwork so that their work could continue, and he could serve his country with honor.

"In this Hell-hole? No f'ing way!" He easily broke free of the men trying to prevent his escape, and the chase had been on. He had managed to get free of the compound for less than an hour. Armed teams had followed him, and when within range, a single shot had caused more alarm than any could have imagined.

The single bullet had found its mark, taking down Edward as it did. And it seemed all hell had indeed broken loose. Tectonic movement of major proportions all around the nation had been reported with varying earthquake ranges. Nevada definitely rumbled. Even little Wisconsin, where Rebecca had been recently hiding out, had felt the effect of that single bullet.

It had been decided that no more attempts at risking Edward's life would be taken. He was slowly, painstakingly nursed back to health, but kept sedated, drugged constantly with morphine. His life became forfeit. Edward would be a hostage. A hostage of his abilities. A hostage of the agency. A hostage of his morphine addiction. Edward's was such a sad case in that sense. He had so much potential, but refused to work with the government.

Much like Rebecca. She, too, had potential, and refused to work with the agency. Very, very few experimentals had emitted signals in their childhood. Most who had were children who had seen terrible accidents or were victims of heinous crimes. Some had them later in life and their ability was triggered by severe trauma or other life-altering events, like a divorce or birth of a child.

Never before had anyone shown as early as Rebecca, nor as strong. Her signals started showing while she was still in the uterus, a fetus! It was baffling to be honest, but throughout her life, life's little big moments made major spikes with Rebecca. Shortly it was discovered that she did most of her spiking while sleeping. Her infant through toddler years confirmed that. Then periodically, she would talk about her weird dreams, and they would coincide with her spiked signals.

Roberts pauses. Quickly he reopens her folder from hard copies from their painstaking rebuilding of lost files, and reads the dictation from one of her visits to the "doctor" at age six. The words leap off the page:

> Her "weird" dreams always are of her "another place," of flying or swimming --without needing to come up for air. She thinks she lives in at least 2 places, and has 2 families.

Slowly he rereads the words. *Another place, two families.* A few pages later he finds another dictation of interest from six months later:

> Rebecca seems to want to share more about her dreams today. Seems her alter-ego is still a version of herself, still Rebecca. But she says she is now hiding from her father. When prompted, she indicates he always seems mad at her.
> Her parents are deeply troubled at that and request we stop asking questions about her dreams. They insist they are not upset with her, and don't know if Rebecca can distinguish the difference. The mom states that once recently, during the dreams, Rebecca called for her, and when she came into the bedroom, she thought Rebecca was floating inches above the bed. When I tried for more information, the mother indicated maybe she was mistaken. Dad was stoic and refused information or insight in any fashion. That is the normal run of events.
> *side note: Rebecca hasn't caught the flu or had cold symptoms in over 3 years even though she currently goes to kindergarten. Will revisit this issue on later visits and verify with school and daycare.

Roberts scanned more pages until he finds one of interest from her pre-teenage years, before they discontinued visits:

> Rebecca brought a few drawings she says are from her dreams. This world is like ours, but she seems to get hostile about that thought. Details are vivid and she gets excited describing what happens, except for the tidal waves that keep coming. She is still saddened by her "dream mother's loss." The father in her dreams seems to have kicked her out on her own,

to fend for herself.

Parents remind me that the current contract doesn't give us any further visitation without their consent after today. They are refusing to give it for future sessions. Will continue to monitor solely via the implant.

Roberts sets the folder down and heads down the fluorescent lit corridor, passing Edward's room before finding the one he wanted. He looks in on her prone figure diminishing day to day since they began the heavy sedation days before. He wasn't too sure he knew what he was about to do, but it was worth a try.

Addressing the nursing assistant monitoring her vitals, he orders, "Wake her up." Seeing her nervous look Roberts almost changes his mind. But too many questions have come up, and now the thought of another Rebecca was too frightening to be sure. Yet, if that was the case, they needed to pursue avenues to protect those at the agency, and the compound.

Especially Edward.

Roberts harrumphs thinking this. Saving Edward from Rebecca.

"Sir?" Roberts hears and looks again through the bullet proof glass protecting him from the prone figure. "Sir? Are you sure about this? You haven't let her wake in three weeks. She hasn't even eaten."

Roberts continues his stare. "I told you to wake her up."

The assistant grimly nods and administers the required medication. Then she lowers the lights, and calls the other nurses to aid her when Rebecca comes to.

Roberts taps his pen lightly on the window frame, his eyes never leaving Rebecca's sleeping face. *Patience was never one of my virtues*, Roberts inwardly grumbles. After fifteen plus minutes of mental images of best and worst case scenarios, he works the kinks out of his neck

and snaps, "How long is this going to freakin' take?"
"Could take another hour or so."
Again, *Patience was never one of my virtues.*

CHAPTER 27

"This is taking forever!" Roberts hollers at the window much later. The lack of acknowledgement for his outburst from the nurse in Rebecca's room reassures him that no one heard him through the tempered glass. His frustration continues to mount as he sees Rebecca's face still in a drugged sleep stupor. Another five minutes go by, and he hits the intercom for the room. "This is taking forever." This time it comes out with a lot more in control.

The tall male nurse looks up and glares at Roberts before turning back to continue his fussing over his charge. "Perhaps you shouldn't have sedated her so thoroughly, Sir."

Roberts wanted to rip the man's head off, but knew he was right. He had ordered her awakened over three hours ago, and nothing had happened. Nothing had changed. She hadn't even flinched, blinked, or swallowed funny. After the first twenty minutes his arm had cramps from hovering above the panic sedation button he had grown so accustomed to pushing. For the next half hour he had stopped even standing above it as he had begun to pace. Now, three hours and twelve minutes into it, he wanted to relieve himself, but was afraid to leave long enough to do so.

A few more minutes go by, and the urge is amplifying itself. Roberts groans.

I can feel her. She hasn't really spoken, but I know Two is here with me. I am so lost and confused. My body feels weak, and I know I don't have the strength to open my eyes. Someone is moving around beside me. Occasionally I can feel a touch or hear movement.

Are you with me? she asks. Her thoughts are sounding like they are so far away, my head is so muffled. But I sense her. Feel her. She is within me.

But I haven't the ability to communicate with her. The energy doesn't even seem to be with me at all. In fact, it is the exact opposite. Like I am being drained. That is the only thought I have. An old movie character's line comes to mind, "Rest, I need rest." Then, like a violent volcano eruption, *I'm gonna hurl.* No energy to even move my body. The nausea continues, then spews forth, and I know I'm choking on it.

Suddenly, my head is turned for me. "It's okay. Let it out." It's a man's voice, deep and calm, and it continues to coo as the burning bile is carefully wiped away. It's not a voice I recognize.

Are you with me now? she asks again. *Can I help you?*

Two. I don't even know if she can hear my thought. It seems so faint. So distant and wispy. My eyes still cannot move. They must be glued shut, or held down with lead or gold. My chest must not even be moving, because a deep breath would take too much effort. Yet, the man continues to work on me. His hands are now wiping my disgusting mess of tangled hair. The cloth is warm, damp, every touch comforting. *Help.*

A gentle "whoosh" and the smallest bit of energy flows. *Boy, what have they done to you?* Though her voice is touched with anger, I am comforted. *Okay, let's open your eyes and see what's what.*

Bright light. Harsh.

And then my eyes are closed again.

Sorry about that, the apology comes instantaneously. *Didn't think they'd open so easily.*

This time, a crack of light. The smallest sliver and my eyelids remain cracked. The light trickles in, and the vague shape of a big man comes in and out of the shadows.

"Are you with us?" he asks carefully.

"She's awake?" That's a voice I had remembered, faintly. It was that Roberts guy, harsh, militant. It sounds of severe static, like through a microphone.

"Only just," comes my attendant's strained voice responds. "Don't get antsy and gas us both."

"She's got a spike," Roberts snarls through the speaker system.

"You wanted her to wake up. She's not even coherent." My guardian quips back. "Do you relish gassing her? Are ya trying to kill the lady?"

They're gassing you.

They're gassing me. They are trying to kill me.

"You don't know what she is capable of," Roberts snaps back.

"Leave me alone." It's my voice. But I didn't say it. I didn't even think of that.

But I did, she informs me quickly.

"Please, don't gas me anymore." Again my voice, but I don't even feel my lips move.

"Her lips aren't moving!" My male protector sputters. "I can hear her, but her lips aren't moving."

My eyes come open more, and blink. This time, I know I am doing it, not Two. Carefully my head rolls to face him. *Don't leave me. Don't let him gas me again. Please.* I make eye contact, try hard not to blink, not to close the heavy lids. *Please.*

"Help me." This passes over my tongue and through my parched lips.

The man continues to hold my gaze, cautious, but he hasn't run away screaming yet. "I am here. Let's get you cleaned up."

"Chris!" Roberts bellows.

The one I assume is Chris turns his big frame towards the sound of Roberts' pitchy temper tantrum. "You wanted her awake. You wanted me to get her ready. I am doing my job. What the hell?"

Two suggests I try to talk only to him, to focus, and see if this Chris is friend or foe. At first my attempts are met with furrowed brow and pursed lips.

He's standing over me again. "Look. Just say what you have to say, or I'll think I'm making all this up," he chastises.

"Hard to," I croak out. "I'm...exhausted, tired. I hurt."

Chris let me know that I had been under the gas' influence for over three straight weeks. My heart sinks. He continues, telling me how my sense of time was far from what was actually true due to the amount of drugging they had done to ensure my safety, and that of everyone at the compound. Frequently he asked me if I would behave, or if they would regret waking me. During all of his questions, I tried to convey my innocence and that I would not be trying to destroy their place of employment. I follow his instructions, and blush horribly when he pulls the IV from my arm and additional tubes out of my bladder and nether regions.

"What a...crappy job," I muse under his critical and cautious eye.

"It's a job," he returns. He puts his hands on his hips, and I take in how big he actually is. He probably should have been a bouncer for his height and build. "Ready to sit up?"

My sense of pride is wounded, but the urge to try is growing. "Sure." *I can't even raise my arm, how am I going to raise my entire torso?*

He offers a small smile that would be almost considered gentle. "I'll help you."

His big arms come around my back, strong to support my weakened being. At his nod and count to three, he practically sat me upright. Okay, he did sit me upright. All by himself. I didn't do any of it, couldn't.

My head instantly spins, and spots dance before me. "I-"

I cannot even finish my thought. The vomit beats the words as I try to turn from him. I didn't miss him completely. Nor did I miss the look of horror as my projectile lands on his pant leg and shoe. He scrunches his face and shakes his head. Carefully he lays me back down and sighs.

"I'm sorry," I mumble.

"Shoulda expected it." Chris shakes his head, "That's what janitors are for."

My eyes close.

That wasn't so bad.

I forgot she was here. *I'm tired.*

I won't be far away. And just so you know, the kids are fine.

With a faint smile, sleep consumes me.

Roberts lowers his hand away from the sedation button as Rebecca sleeps again. Luckily he hadn't needed to press the panic button despite her spike. A quick glance at the monitor tells him that the spike isn't so much a spike anymore. It's become more of a constant hum, like it had been the last three weeks, minus a few hours here and there.

"So you didn't need to gas us?"

Roberts looks at the man standing next to a pool of green bile. "Not this time," he announces in the microphone. "Can never be too sure with Rebecca."

Chris looks over at the sleeping figure. "Yep, a terror. Now, can you let me out? I have to change. And this place needs to get cleaned up. It reeks in here."

Roberts buzzes the lock.

Bureau of Federal Energy and Interest   NRG-ASE

Case #: R00013ASE   Case Name: Rebecca
DOB: 07/23/1974   Code: energy

CLASSIFIED

Observation time/date: 4 December 2008/1617hrs
Report type: Weekly follow-up
Time in observation: 48 days
Weight: 144lbs
Status: semi-alert
Method of medication: NA

Notes:

Rebecca (Case #: R00013ASE) was removed from sedation per Roberts' orders. Subject has lessened motor skills, atrophy, and vomited.

Energy levels from the subject have been detected since subject has been revived.

Review of tapes continues to show despondent behavior. Only word spoken since shown to her quarters is "to". Limited dialog with contact, but not with physicians or Roberts, when present in subject's quarters. Chris has volunteered to assist as necessary.

Bureau of Federal Energy and Interest

DD Form 99-ASE   BFEI-USA   Subject Record

CHAPTER 28

It has been three days since I woke up. Three days since time came crashing down on me. Three painstaking days of simple broths and juices and lots of naps. Three days of near constant assistance from Chris, and two other nurses when he isn't around. It was worse than fighting any flu. There was never a chance of my situation getting better. No sense of hope or purpose. My only highlights were feeling Two, and our silent conversations. Her plans on breaking me out of this mental and physical prison. Her letting me know another implant was now "installed" as she called it. Her letting me know what Jay and Joanna were doing when they "visited."

Today was October 29th, or so I was being told. Could it possibly be true? Could almost two months of my life had already passed me by?

A glance in the two-way mirror tells me that it was definitely possible. The dark circles under my eyes are a true testament of my lack of nutrition. My weakened legs and arms a remark on my length of continued unconscious existence. My body no longer held itself with bearing. Now it feels like a limp sail, awaiting the stiff breeze to encourage movement, and sustain it.

Part of me wants to thank this agency for helping me shed the unwanted pounds I learned I had lost. The other part feels hot, angry. How dare they violate my health and safety that way! Chris told me earlier this morning when they helped me to the scale that I have lost a total of "eighteen-and-a-half" pounds. My legs had buckled hearing that. Yes, definitely the energy allowed me to feel hot and angry.

Most of the time I feel so alone.

But now, I sit before what I can only name as my nemesis. Roberts. The simple tiled walls remind me of those that would be on those police shows during interrogations.

"This place isn't very homey," I mumble.

Roberts regards me a moment, then glances back on the page of my file he had been reading. A few more moments of pregnant silence continues as he reads, then rereads the passage. Then he brings out his pen, formulates a question, and speaks it. "Who is this other person you see yourself being?"

My mind races. "I am not sure I understand the question."

He looks at me a moment, then purses his lips in vexation. "You have dreams; have since you were a child. You have referred to this as another you, another place, with another family. What can you tell me about that?"

My mouth needs to be closed before I can regain my composure. Idly my fingers pick at the thread on my inmate shirt. "I don't know how to explain it. It just is...another me, someplace else. As a kid, I thought she was like an imaginary friend only to be found in my dreams when I slept. She looks like me. Talks like me. But the place is different..."

"A different country?" he prods.

My look must have taken him off guard. "Definitely not."

Roberts rolls his eyes and waves his hand, "Another *world* perhaps?" His sarcasm drips like thick syrup.

It irritates me. "I don't know."

'He sighs in his irritation with me. "Are you trying to convince me you are dreaming of an alien planet?"

My turn for sarcasm. "Did I say it was an alien planet?"

He taps his pen again. "Look, Rebecca, I..."

"Don't call me that," I interrupt.

His look is cautious. "Don't call you what?" He pauses a moment. "Rebecca?"

"Yes," I hold his look.

"Why? It's your name, isn't it? Rebecca?" He actually seems confused, baffled really.

"If you cannot treat me like a person, don't call me by my name." My eyes bore into his. I can feel Two ready to help me offer him a glimpse as to what he has done to me, not just the past two-and-a-half months, but the past two plus years of hell and anguish. "My name is Rebecca, but to my friends. You are definitely not my friend."

That damn pen taps again. "Okay." He chews the inside of his lip a moment. Then settles back a bit in his chair while he assesses me. His scrutiny is met with my hard resolve. "Change of subject..."

"Yes! I am outta here," I try to stand with some sense of authority.

"Sit down," he states simply as the pen tat-tat-tats on the desk between us. "Why are you being so damned difficult about this?" His hard eyes hold mine in their iciness.

Shock. That is the first thing that I feel hearing that sentence come so vehemently from that man's mouth. "Really?" I hear myself offer in my shock. "You can really ask that as you sit there tapping your frickin' pen? After how you have treated me. Not just today, but *both* times I have been in your *care*." His eyes continue his cool stare. "You can. Seriously? Wow." I shake my head, breaking his stare down. "I wish I could explain it to you." My eyes retry meeting his. "I really do."

That damn pen! "Please do," he challenges.

"I don't know how. It's all in my head. Images. Memories."

Show him, she suggests.

It's a good idea, but...

Do it, she all but commands.

I can feel the energy, feel it coax me, comfort me. I look into Robert's face, his bored eyes and lips pressed tight. "All right, but you asked for it." And I project the beginning of this whole ordeal starting over two years ago with a man named Adam who interviewed me, followed by the whole being on the run and hiding, minus Jay Strebeck's involvement of course. I emphasize the pain from my surgery, the fear of family's safety, fear of my safety and that of my own mental health, the loss of my husband and marriage, and the pain involved making the decision both times to turn myself into the agency, and for what? This harassment? This anguish? This mistreatment and constant negativity? I let him see himself as I see him, and aptly have labeled him. My nemesis. A small smile of pride reaches my lips as I see how that stings him.

Then letting all of my bombardment of emotions and past settle upon him, I challenge, *How can you even sleep at night? How can you face your loved ones?*

Silence consumes the both of us, while I feel the energy work around my foe, this Roberts. My eyes slowly lower as I think about how much I have shared. *Perhaps I shouldn't have shared all of that with him.*

He asked for it.

But, I gave in. I let him win. I let the energy do what he wanted to see happen.

True. But he needed to see what he has done to you. Done to your life. And the life of your kids.

I miss them.

I know.

He clears his throat, and looks down. His pen is shoved aside. "Did I just imagine all of that? Or..."

"That is how I lived, how my life was during..." I snap in defense.

His raised hand cuts me off. "Not that. I got that. Loud and clear." His face contorts a brief moment. "Were you just talking about me? To yourself?"

Shit!

Quiet!

"No," my voice quavers a brief second. "That is my other self, my other me. The one I dream about." My eyes flicker towards the two-way mirror. "She is the reason your Frankenstein scientist doctor is freaking out in the other room." My eyes meet his. "When we meet, talk, dream, whatever you want to call it, the energy between us is intense, amplified. I can hear her, feel her. And she me."

"What's her name? This other her person-thingy?" Roberts seems genuinely interested, and a bit concerned.

"Well, you won't be able to say it. She feels the same as I do on the subject."

"What subject?" he queries cautiously, reaching for his pen.

Mentally I snatch the pen from his reaching fingers with a glance. It flicks into my awaiting hand in what feels like a second. A small smile pulls at my lips. The energy is all around me. It has come so easy, like I have never stopped with it. My eyes reach his as my smile lingers.

"Her name is Rebecca."

His chair hits the floor as he tries to exit the room.

Bureau of Federal Energy and Interest   NRG-ASE

Case #: R00013ASE   Case Name: Rebecca
DOB: 07/23/1974   Code: energy

CLASSIFIED

Observation time/date: 5 December 2008/1100hrs
Report type: Weekly follow-up
Time in observation: 49 days
Weight: 143lbs
Status: alert
Method of medication: NA

Notes:

Rebecca (Case #: R00013ASE) Subject still has lessened motor skills.

Serious energy levels from the subject have been detected since subject has been revived. Due to atrophy, rehabiliatation commenced.

Roberts has others doe interrogations and interviews with subject, but subject no longer interacts in such sessions. Roberts has pushed nurse Chris to seek information and "befriend" the subject.

Bureau of Federal Energy and Interest

DD Form 99-ASE   BFEI-USA   Subject Record

CHAPTER 29

"Where have you been?" Shadow's worried voice is so welcome and almost foreign it has been so long since I have heard it. "Derk and I have been worried sick!" Yet, she continues to advance in her deep pregnant waddle towards me as I sit up. "You have been...well, gone! Like you were dead, but asleep or comatose! We've been extremely worried! Again!"

I cannot help but give her a huge hug to calm her babble. "I am sorry." It's all I can muster at the moment. I may have been asleep the past few days, but I am just exhausted. "I had to go. She needed me. Still does. Once I found her, I had to be sure she was safe."

Derk's loving arms wrap around me. My own personal cocoon of comfort. "And is she?"

My lips find his. "Yes, for now." Carefully I withdraw from my husband's hug. "They had her so drugged and sedated. She was ill. She hadn't been fed or anything in days. Weeks. Some guy from some government agency..."

"Like before," Shadow finishes my partial thought.

"Yes," I nod. "She turned herself over to them to protect her kids' lives. The people she turned herself over to don't trust her. Seems when I found her, they sedated her to the point of comatose. They had tubes going all over, in and out, just keeping her alive and yet barely functioning. Tubes to verify air flow. Tubes for her urine, and another to keep her hydrated. Tubes for feeding her. Speaking of that, I am starving."

Derk hurries off with a "Food coming right up!"

Shadow frowns, "She was really as bad off as all that?"

"When have you ever known me to lie?" My eyebrows challenge her though my lips are curved in a smile. Seeing she's in no joking mood, I nod solemnly. "It wasn't pretty. She got sick a lot coming out of it. It took days her time." Seeing it is dark outside I venture to ask how long I have been out helping my other self.

Shadow wrings her hands in her lap. "Normally I wouldn't have been so worried. I know you go off and do your own dream thing. I know sometimes your sense of time isn't the same in your dreams."

Her rambling worries me. "How long?"

Her shoulders drop. "Almost two weeks."

"Two weeks?" My voice cracks. I thought it had been three days since I found her with the kids' help and decided to tell them I was going to see if I could help her. That I had made a promise to Jay and Joanna. "Two weeks?" I ask again to her awaiting nod. "Odd. That's how long it's been there since she woke up. She's fought going to sleep at all for fear they'd drug her again. I finally convinced her she needed her rest, and that I needed to get back."

Two weeks.

"Two weeks." My voice cracks as I look at Shadow and Derk. "Well," I smile brightly, trying to whisk myself into standing and the appearance of normalcy, "I guess it's time I get a move on then."

Derk holds out a hand to help me. "Seriously? You've been like a corpse for two whole weeks, and you wake up like nothing has happened. Like you haven't been causing me...us, grief and worry?"

The alarm in his voice cuts through me, takes the happy-go-lucky from my movements. Suddenly, I feel like

I'm pushing through thick, overwhelming mud while moving. I lose my bearing and pause. Slowly, I turn to him. "I'm sorry to have caused you, both of you," never looking up, "pain and grief and worry." All that has transpired in my counterpart's life comes bubbling forth. I sit there, shaking my head. "I know this isn't what you signed up for Derk." My mind races to her past, and the knowledge that her husband has left her under similar circumstances. "I know this is a lot to take on, that you never wanted a life like this..."

His hand goes out and covers my mouth, "Don't put words in my mouth."

Already I smile, my hand touching his arm, as I interject, "Sorry." Tenderly I run my fingers down the length of his arm, following his sleeve to his wrist, then running my fingers gingerly over his fingers. "I know that, Derk. I do. I also know how we met." I can still see in his eyes the wharf, the mystical dance that I just couldn't stop from happening, the shun of the crowd at the climax of the when a man slid between my legs in an erotic, sexual posturing. Derk was there. He was one of the men I manipulated for that dance in front of all the town's people who thought they were so above me. He had followed me. Followed Shadow and me. I had to shut him out to absolve him of his social crimes in the town's eyes, when he followed with me, talked to me...looked at me. "Derk, you know I love you, have since that day. I know you have had to put up with so much...so much."

Derk tenderly kisses my wandering fingers. "I'd do it again, and again." He looks into my eyes, and I feel the depth of emotions echoing in his eyes. "You made me wake up. I have never...never, ever felt so...alive, as I do with you. Here and now, from the moment I have met you, until now, here in this moment." He slowly shakes his head, "Even knowing some of these words seem not like my own, I know them to be mine." He smiles genuinely and kisses my fingertips, "I know I do love you. I do that my life with you has been touched by...something. Something otherworldly. And, I do know that loving you means I love the you that is trapped somewhere else. I know you are more than complicated. It's just...I feel trapped sometimes."

My heart stops. "That's it! She's trapped! She's allowed herself to be trapped! They keep putting her to sleep when I visit." Seeing their perplexed looks, "They knock her out!" My hand frantically scratches at my head in annoyance. "They are making her a lab rat!"

Shadow frowns more and steps closer to me. "Maybe then you shouldn't seek her out."

I look up at her in disbelief. "How can you say that? You know she's now incarcerated, and yet I'm her only true hope for freedom."

Shadow looks straight at me. "Maybe it would be best to leave her alone for a while. Let her fight her own battles. Let whoever it is who is watching her see there is nothing to worry about."

That is why I love her so much. She is my not so silent voice of logic. I bow my head and smile sadly. "I have thought of that, yes." My eyes find hers, and I send her an instant mental update on all I know and have felt, like a video clip of my time with my...other me. I watch as it all plays on my dearest friend's face, and I have to look away. I know how painful all of this has been for her through the years. Being my best and dearest friend, okay, honestly, my only friend for most of my life, has come with the most serious price tag. Not only had I hid her from people for years, I have had to "download" to her, sharing everything, every intimate detail for years and years as we grew up. Only she knows me so well. It hurts her to know what I feel and know. I know that, and so does she. What we both know what hurts more is her true pain experiencing it firsthand when I do this to her.

Part of me feels guilty. Part of me needs her to back me up. To support me, and my other self, go through this, in that foreign place she lives. Part of me lingers in the other world in that moment when I send Shadow everything she needs to know to understand where I am, in this moment, with both of them looking at me like I am nuts.

Slowly, Shadow closes her eyes. And she softly sighs.

Derk looks at her and snorts, "What? Again? Anything for me, or is it all for her again?"

Shadow puts her hand out to him and shakes her head, "You don't want this."

"Maybe I do!" He stands up and stomps away, only to turn sharply. "I agreed to this. I opened myself to you. I took you to be my *wife*!" He turns his back on me and runs his fingers through his hair.

I cannot deny his involvement. Only his resolve. Gently, knowing Shadow shakes her head, I touch his mind, letting him in. I let the images flow. From my first real understanding of my connection to her, my other self, to now, I let him see. Feel. Understand. I look up to watch his shoulders tense, then drop, only to tense and drop several times. It all lasts maybe seconds, maybe minutes, maybe an hour, but now Derk knows. He knows me at my most intimate. He knows my weaknesses and secrets. He fully and finally understands, and has the insight to reflect on, the whole of me. I look down, unsure of his response. I am briefly aware of Shadow's hand on mine.

I focus on that, and can hear the heartbeat of her daughter within her, strong and true. Again the guilt plagues me, knowing how many people are attached to this other version of me. Tears tempt my eyes, and I shut out the urge.

"Why do these people care?"

I look into Derk's eyes. He's faced me squarely and meets my gaze with no emotion behind them. I shrug.

"They are holding her, and others. For what purpose?" His look and posturing show how pissed off he truly is, though his voice is calm and...calculated.

I hold his look. "I don't know." I look out the window after a second, remembering someone from long ago. "I think they think of her...us...as a weapon."

Shadow chimes loudly, "Like hell!!"

Derk comes forward, his stance makes me look at

him anew. "What kind of weapon?"
 I shrug. "A dangerous one?"

Bureau of Federal Energy and Interest   NRG-ASE

Case #: R00013ASE   Case Name: Rebecca
DOB: 07/23/1974   Code: energy

CLASSIFIED

Observation time/date: 8 December 2008/1203hrs
Report type: Weekly follow-up
Time in observation: 52 days
Weight: 144lbs
Status: conscious
Method of medication: NA

Notes:

Rebecca (Case #: R00013ASE) continues to recuperate after Roberts ordered her to be awakened. Due to lack of activity, subject has lessened motor skills ans is still very weak. Rehab has continued, x3 daily.

Limited levels from the subject have been detected since subject has been revived. She will be allowed consciousness until activity is deemed unsafe.

Subject still refuses most conversation and activity. She has spoken briefly with male attendant, Chris, throughout the past three days. Perhaps will try to have Chris assist with evaluations.

Rebecca looks at the two-way mirror as if she can see the observers, doctors. She seems to know when they are in the room, and where they are. Energy spikes are noted with this as well.

Bureau of Federal Energy and Interest

DD Form 99-ASE   BFEI-USA   Subject Record

CHAPTER 30

Can you hear me now?
Suddenly I am awake. Every fiber of my being straining to see in the dark cell I am held captive in. My eyes blink against the darkness, reaching and pulling out the vague shapes and shadows almost familiar. I know I heard it, faint, but very present. Like someone had been in my cell. I can't really think of it as my room. Cell fits better. Captive of a willing person to save my family. Cell all the same.
Can you? A small pause. *Can you?* A squeal, like a mouse squeak or something.
I sit upright, then I quickly relax, knowing my every movement is being watched and recorded. Chris had assured me that two long months ago. Yet they had not even questioned me or anything. Chris had told me they were trying to "Discern my volatility." Whatever that meant. I just know that I had slept for way too long. I knew that because I had lost weight, a lot of weight. I also couldn't move when I woke up. It was like my body wasn't my own. Chris had told me that it was my body being in a state of atrophy. That didn't even seem to make sense at first. But after a few weeks' worth of therapy, which consisted of Chris moving all of my limbs against my not so slight verbal onslaught of complaints, and my

actual tears of pain and upset, I had limited range of motion on my own. Slowly, painfully, I sat up and swung my legs over the edge of the cot "they" called a bed. Gingerly, I tilted my head back to ease the muscles there, then helped by rubbing my neck with my left hand. My right hand gripped the feeble framing in case I heard the question again.

Hearing nothing, I slowly stand, working the kinks out like Chris has taught me. I didn't leave the side of the bed for fear my knees shaking would allow my collapse to the cold floor below. Again, I slowly rub my neck muscles...and into the shoulder muscles.

One last time, can you hear me?

I gasp and quickly fall to the cot. Quickly I work out my legs, pretending that is why I sat so quickly. Softly, almost to myself, I offer, "Yes."

Silence.

Silence so long I think I must have imagined it. I know I haven't ever heard that voice before. It's definitely not Two. That I know for two reasons. First, Two is calm, reassuring...me, and like me. Second, this was a male's voice. Quiet, like a whisper, desperate to be heard. Hard, but uncertain. A man's voice. My mind races over voices I've heard and I am quite sure I've never heard this one before.

Still silence.

Maybe I hadn't answered soon enough.

Maybe I should have said it in my head. Used my thoughts.

Maybe I hadn't heard anything in the first place.

Maybe this place was making me crazy. Making me imagine things that really weren't.

Probably.

I know I gasped. I heard it. Panic set in me. I don't want to be gassed again. I don't want them to put me out, not when someone was trying to communicate with me. My mind races. *Don't let them know. Don't let them know.* And quickly I rubbed my legs, all the way down the ankles. I carefully look around my dark and shadow-filled

cell. *Look normal. Look normal.* Nothing stands out as unusual. No Boogie Man. No Night Demons. No one. Nothing.
 Finally.
 I look around again.
 It's okay. I promise. Sleep.

 School buses were dropping us off at our school nestled amongst the pines and near a hill. The sun was shining. Slinging my backpack over my right shoulder I walked into the building looking around. Part of me knew I had never been here before, ever. The other part knew it was just another day at school, happy, go-lucky, walking the halls, trying not to get hit with wandering spit balls, or notes that get attached to someone's backpack that say "KICK ME." Just put my head down and push through and get to class.
 Where am I going?
 As soon as I thought that, my feet seem to take to the halls with a memory I had not known. Smelly lockers. Overly perfumed teenaged bodies. Hairspray wafting in the air. High school all over again. Dang it.
 Funny.
 I squint at the weird male voice in my head. Shaking my head, continue on.
 Boring classes.
 Gross lunch of chicken pasta and slimy green beans.
 Off to more boring classes.
 Ready?
 I glance at the kids pushing through the halls with me for just a moment. *Whatever.* I push between some dude and some chick getting their flirt on. *Whatever.* My favorite phrase, yet so appropriate as I navigate my high school halls. I'm heading towards... Science? How do I know that? Why is that important?
 BOOOOOOM!
 The whole school shakes. Panic reverberates, then ensues. I'm afraid, and then I see the wall of fire as it

envelopes me.

Again.

School buses were dropping us off. The sun was shining. I walked into the building looking around. Part of me knew I had never been here before. The other part knew it was just another day at school, happy, go-lucky, walking the halls, trying not to get hit with wandering spit balls, or notes that get attached to someone's backpack that say "KICK ME." Just put my head down and push through and get to class.
Where am I going?
As soon as I thought that, my feet seem to take to the halls with a memory I had not known. Smelly lockers. Overly perfumed teenaged bodies. Hairspray wafting in the air. High school all over again.
Boring classes.
Gross lunch of some chicken dish and limp veggies.
More boring classes.
Ready?
I glance at the kids pushing through the halls with me for just a moment. *Whatever.* I push between some dude and some chick getting their flirt on. *Whatever.* My favorite phrase, yet so appropriate as I navigate my high school halls. I'm heading towards... Science? How do I know that? Why is that important?
BOOOOOOM!
The whole school shakes. Panic reverberates, then ensues. I'm afraid, and then I see the wall of fire as it envelopes me. Didn't I just do this?

Again.

School buses were dropping us off. The sun was shining. I walked into the building looking around. Part of me knew I had never been here before. The other part knew it was just another day at school, happy, go-lucky, walking the halls, trying not to get hit with wandering spit balls, or notes that get attached to someone's backpack that say "KICK ME." Just put my head down and push through and get to class.

Where am I going?

As soon as I thought that, my feet seem to take to the halls with a memory I had not known. Smelly lockers. Overly perfumed teenaged bodies. Hairspray wafting in the air. High school all over again.

Boring classes.

Gross lunch of something someone dares call chicken and veggies.

More boring classes.

Ready?

I glance at the kids pushing through the halls with me for just a moment. *Whatever.* I push between some dude and some chick getting their flirt on. *Whatever.* My favorite phrase, yet so appropriate as I navigate my high school halls. I'm heading towards... Science? How do I know that? Why is that important? Why is this seeming familiar? I feel like I'm supposed to know something? Do something?

BOOOOOOM!

The whole school shakes. Panic reverberates, then ensues. I'm afraid, and then I see the wall of fire as it envelopes me.

Again.

School buses were dropping us off. The sun was shining. I walked into the building looking around. Part of me knew I had never been here before. The other part knew it was just another day at school, happy, go-lucky, walking the halls, trying not to get hit with wandering spit balls, or notes that get attached to someone's backpack that say "KICK ME." Just put my head down and push through and get to class.

Where am I going?

As soon as I thought that, my feet seem to take to the halls with a memory I had not known. Smelly lockers. Overly perfumed teenaged bodies. Hairspray wafting in the air. High school all over again. But this time, a sense of déjà vu.

Funny.

I squint at the weird male voice in my head. Shaking my head, continue on.

Boring classes.

Gross lunch.

More boring classes.

Ready?

I glance at the kids pushing through the halls with me for just a moment. *Whatever.* I push between some dude and some chick getting their flirt on. *Whatever.* My favorite phrase, yet so appropriate as I navigate my high school halls. I'm heading towards...Science? How do I know that? Why is that important? Man, this really feels redundant. I know I've done this before. I know I've heard of déjà vu before. I know this is it. It's now screaming in my ears. Why can't anyone else sense this is wrong? Something bad is going to happen.

I stop, looking around for a sign. A door going outside, the wire-enforced glass window beckons. How can I say "No?" I touch the door, look back at those meandering to class. To those casting me weird looks. I push on the fire exit bar of the door, nervous, but willing to take the heat from the Principal.

BOOOOOOM!

The whole school shakes. Panic reverberates, then ensues. I'm afraid, and then I see the wall of fire as it envelopes me.

Again.

Another Time

School buses were dropping us off. The sun was shining. I walked into the building looking around. *What? Wait a minute! What's going on? I know this.* I look around. *Screw this. I'm not going in. Kiss mine.*

A couple of people look at me and proceed into the building. Not me. I'm going to wait out in the sunshine, smelling the trees. Make them come get me.

The bells ring starting the day. They keep time with the classes throughout the day.

My tummy grumbles in complaint for missing what I know would have been a crappy lunch. Probably some chicken or pasta. Or some nasty combination of the two. Oh, and a side of some limp vegetables. Can't forget that.

I wonder what I am missing.

BOOOOOOM!

The whole school shakes. Panic reverberates, then ensues. I'm afraid, and then I see the wall of fire as it engulfs the school and all its faculty and students, except me.

Again.

School buses were dropping us off. The sun was shining.

Stop! What the hell? I know I've done this before. Like just freakin' before. I look around and know I'm right. Same clothes. Same understanding of classes. What happens? What is up? Why is this wrong? The whole thing. It's wrong.

Shit!

I run into the school screaming about a bomb. Through my hysterics I tell them that it's going to happen shortly after lunch. "We have to get everyone out of here!"

I'm looking at my teachers' faces. They are familiar, yet not. Someone grabs me and holds me in place and another comes in front of me trying to calm me. All day I sit in the office, panicking when the officers come in to talk with me, ask me how I know, hold me in a cold unseeing room while the day goes on.

BOOOOOOM!

The whole school shakes. Panic reverberates, then ensues. I'm afraid, and then I see the wall of fire as it envelopes me.

Again.

School buses were dropping us off. The sun was shining. I walked into the building looking around. Part of me knew I had done this at least five times before. Seems like a dozen. But this time I remember, but I know I cannot tell the school staff. They won't believe me. Well, they don't know how I know. They want to blame me for a scheme.

I'm trying to protect you!

I look around and see a familiar face. I enlist her help. Tell her after lunch, we need to do a mock fire drill, and run out the fire doors. Somehow I convince her. She has a few friends who believe us and think it'll be cool. Who cares about getting suspended?

After lunch, we head to the doors. Weird. Same doors as before.

I look back. Not many of us.

I look at the doors, and push them open and run for the pine trees and slight decline ahead. People are laughing as they follow me. They don't get it. But this time I have saved some. This time will be different. All the previous attempts flash in my mind.

BOOOOOOM!

The whole school shakes. Panic reverberates amongst us outside the school. I'm afraid, and then I see the wall of fire as it ruptures through the doors we just vacated.

Again.

School buses were dropping us off. The sun was shining. I walked into the building looking around. *Wait a second.* I step back outside, déjà vu is so strong. Then I see it all happen.
STOP!
Part of me knows what has to be done.
I know I have until just after lunch. I don't go to class. I skip, looking for any sign of problems. Any sign of a disturbed person. I hang out in the gymnasium, knowing this is the last place I have yet to check before the bomb or bombs go off.
I have found the gymnasium, and know the moment as I look into the detonator's eyes.
Damn it. I run, screaming, *"NOOOOO!"*
BOOOOOOM!
The whole school shakes. I never even see the wall of fire as it envelopes me in that brief second.

Again.

School buses were dropping us off. The sun was shining. I walked into the building looking around. Part of me knew I had just done this over a dozen times.
What am I missing? What the crap?!
I stop in front of the doors. People shoulder me and try to knock me through the front doors of that quiet, peaceful school. I knew better. I knew it was going to blow up shortly after lunch. I stand watching the last of the teachers and students enter as I replayed the last fourteen, fifteen, sixteen times that I remember I have entered this school. I have stayed outside. I have tried saving a few of the students, different students each time, and even some of the teachers. I have been under arrest for a bomb threat only to watch it go up in smoke and flames. I have tried to

stop the person from setting off the bomb in the gymnasium three times, only to die each time. Something I was doing was wrong.

What is it that I need to do?

I know when. I know who. I know how to survive. I have tried to save people. What am I supposed to do?

I look up at the partly cloudy sky and sigh.

The answer hits me like the bomb that's about to go off. I know I have to save everyone.

But how?

I walk into the school, looking for anything to help me.

There it is. A beacon. A lifeboat.

I am so dumb. I curse myself. I make a mental note of how many beacons I pass, and their locations. After a lunch I know I have only two things to face. Another time in this high school hell, or finally my crappy lunch will pass through my bowels.

Boring classes.

Gross lunch, of...oh yeah, some crappy pasta with chicken chunks. Yum.

More boring classes.

Ready?

Walk up to the beacon. I have about five minutes, more or less. It has always varied a bit.

Swallowing, I pull it and run to the fire doors. Water falls. Sirens and bells blare. Students and teachers pour out of classrooms. I make for the fire doors, pushing through, running like everyone else, but I keep running. Away from the panic and mayhem. Away from the screams. Away from the all too familiar smell of charred bodies. Away from this nightmare that won't ever, ever end.

BOOOOOOM!

I stop, turn around and look. People, lots of people are out this time. Lots. More than ever before. Someone is on fire in front of me. I run forward and jump on him, tackling his screaming body to the ground, patting out the flames on his clothes. I'm screaming that it'll be alright,

that I got it right this time. His panicked look does nothing to help me as I swat at the lingering fiery fingers of doom.
Don't worry. I've got this.

I hope you do.

I wake up, looking around. I'm lying on my cot, dripping sweat. I haven't been gassed into unconsciousness. I am alive. More importantly, there is no bomb.

CHAPTER 31

Chris sits in my sessions, like some sort of support. I'm not sure if it's for me or them. Part of me is grateful to not be in these alone, but I know why he's here. He's here to restrain me and sedate me if need be. I know this, not only because he told me, but he's tapping his thigh with the syringe again. It's very annoying. He told me he didn't want to do this; that he didn't want to be the bad guy. He told me the agency thinks I need a "friend" here, to make it easier on myself. Personally, I think that sounds like him talking, and he was convincing enough to make it happen. He's a big and burly man to be sure, at about six feet four inches, but on our few times of talking I learned he has a huge heart, a good heart.

The "panel" sits on the opposite side of the table. Three people: Roberts, and two medical-looking people who have never introduced themselves. They ask questions, watch my face and scribble on their pads. Most times Roberts does most of the asking. And it's stupid stuff. It reminds me of the last time, years ago, when I underwent their interrogations and "testing."

Roberts tries every session to take command of the room. I don't know if he thinks that intimidates me or what. Like I need to be intimidated. I'm still weak. Chris and another one of three staff members come in three times a day to help me move. I know they think it's necessary. I just wish they'd all stop touching me. They have me feeling helpless. But I guess they all know I'm not, or Roberts wouldn't be giving me the stare-down. And Chris wouldn't be tapping his thigh with that syringe.

"Well?" Roberts is raising an eyebrow, like he's waiting for something.

I glance around and see all of them are looking at me that way. "I'm sorry. What?"

He sighs loudly, and taps his pencil on the open file in front of him. "I asked you if you're ready to work with us. Help us to trust one another."

I digest what he has said. My eyes me his, and I try to keep mine blank. "You have yet to show me I can trust you."

He snorts and thrusts his pen forward like a dagger. "We are taking necessary precautions. You are dangerous."

"All trapped things can be dangerous."

Chris stifles a chuckle. The note takers are scribbling away.

"So you admit we can't trust you."

"I admitted no such thing. As I recall I let myself be taken here. I, in turn, have been gassed to the point of non-existence by you. Held captive, no room, clock, clothing of my own. I have you trying to kill me, and you are wondering if you can trust me? I haven't even tried to defend myself against your...interests." I try to keep my anger from flaring, afraid Chris will stab me and I'll be left a drooling rag doll. "I understand you feel whatever it is I do is...or can be, dangerous. I haven't robbed a bank. I haven't gone out and murdered people..."

"What about the other compound? The one you destroyed?" Roberts barks.

My eyes hold his, then I drop mine. "Then I guess you should start treating me nicely." My eyes flicker up to his again. *I should not have said that*, I chastise myself.

The note takers whisper amongst themselves briefly while Roberts and I hold each other's stares. One makes Roberts break his look as he turns to listen to the whisperer, and the whisperer next to him.

"Secrets don't make friends." My eyes look around the room now instead. "They breed enemies and lies. I tried to teach my kids that." I glance towards the chuckling Chris once again. "Well, it's true."

He nods, "I know."

"Let me ask you something. Did everyone die?" I'm back to looking at Roberts. "Seems I was told, or heard, that there were survivors." I roll my eyes as more whispers.

"Clearly you weren't listening. Too wrapped up in your little gossipy chat."

Roberts finally turns and looks at me. "Sorry?"

"Whatever," I mumble. I won't look back their way now. I'm much too interested in how many rivets are along the doorway seams, and the corners' seams. I look at the ones around the two-way mirror. "So I was asked back then to do parlor tricks. I was threatened and about to be tortured. The way I see it, I was acting in self-defense." My eyes catch a missing rivet. Nothing here is perfect. "The negative energy there, the pain and memories there...that's what caused the destruction of your precious compound." My eyes notice again the slight scratches on the two-way mirror glass. "So, in essence, you killed those people. Minus any survivors." My eyes meet Roberts. "There were survivors."

Chris shifts in the silence that follows. Long, heavy seconds. No blinking. Just Chris trying to break the tension and end the silence.

"So I understand, from what you've told me, I send and receive signals. You're soooo funny. It's not necessarily signals. It's energy, the stuff all around us. That's why I'm coded as 'energy,' right? Because you almost get it? Well, let me assure you that even I don't get it. I don't get how I can hear her, Two, and sometimes you can. I don't know why this is a matter of national interest or security or whatever. I just know it when I feel it. And I can feel it. I can hear it. And in my dreams I can harness it.

"I've always been told it's rare to dream in color. That's so odd to me. It's all I ever do. It's how I have always dreamt. It's also odd to me that I can have a dream over and over and over and over, knowing I have to figure it out like a puzzle, but others don't. I can have whole months pass by in my dreams, -"

"Your other world...," Roberts chimes in, so I shoot him a dirty look, then go back to the walls and rivets.

"Didn't anyone ever tell you not to interrupt?" I shake my head. "I can have a whole month *there*, wherever that is, and wake up here and only an hour has passed. I don't get how I can eat, sleep, walk, I do a lot of walking, piss, and have dreams there for a few weeks or a month, if I'm just dreaming for an hour here." A wistful smile comes to my face and I can feel it, moving now. "Maybe you should be the ones being checked out. Maybe you all are dumb or something. They say smart people use more of their brains." I meet Robert's eyes again, "At least I can honestly say I'm using mine."

Poor Chris can't hold it in and earns a stern look from Roberts, who looks at my file and tries to collect himself. "Give me a recent example of one of these dreams, if you can."

So, in vivid, slow detail, I tell him about my recent school dream, the bomb, and reliving it, over and over. I make sure he knows I can smell, touch, taste, run...and die, with every version. I add in hearing my narrative of "Again" and "Better." The silence is deafening, so I look back at the "panel." Clearly they seem alarmed about what I've just disclosed. "What?" I glance back at Chris. "What's up?"

Finally, I hear the voice of one of the panel. "You said it was a man's voice?" At my nod, "One you've not heard before?" At my nod, the whispering commences yet again. I look to Chris for an answer but only receive a shrug. One scribbler quickly gets up and leaves the room, firmly securing the door behind him.

Roberts closes my file and the speaking scribbler does the same. Roberts casts a quick, "Take her back, please, Chris."

Chris stands with me and heads toward the door, waiting for it to open, as has become standard for these sessions. "Come on." Still tapping that stupid syringe against his thigh as we go.

We navigated the sterile hallways back to my prison cell.

"It's not a prison cell." Chris sighs.

"Excuse me?" I hadn't even tried to project my thoughts. My eyes dart to the syringe.

"You talk about all this like it's a prison." He rolls his head back. "It's not really." He holds my door open. "It's more like a medical hospital."

"Oh, like a lab, and I'm some rat to be tested."

Again his deep sigh, "No, that's not right either. I guess you can see it that way because you're...the rat." He shuts the door behind me, as has become ritual. "We found the others, the 'experimentals', in these membranes, when the other site was leveled. Like they were in weird cocoons. It seemed impossible. All that destruction. And yet, I personally found two, safe and sound. At first we didn't know how to get them out, but they did it themselves. They just...woke up, and the cocoons would...disappear." He looked at me. "It's been said that you did that. Made the cocoons. Protected them. I bet hearing your dream that you had to do over and over made them all paranoid again."

"But I didn't want to redo the dream. It just happens. Most of the time I get the challenge, the puzzle, within a few redos. But that one took forever!"

Chris sets the syringe down and took what we call "his seat" in the only chair in the room. I sit on my cot. "Do you always have someone narrating them?"

"No, this was the first time."

Chris scrunches his face again. "When you were...with...us the last time, did you meet any of the others?"

"No. I wasn't there long. Two came and rescued me." I look at the gaps in the acrylic tile on the floor under my feet. "I knew what had happened there. I was taken to a torture chamber of sorts, and that was that. We were done. All that pain and punishment for what? Having a brain?"

"Do you honestly think you use your brain more than other people? Normal people?" He's all settled and sprawled into "his seat" now. I guess he's planning on being here awhile.

"I don't know. I can't speak for others, nor myself. I've never been tested that way." I think a moment. "At least not that I know of."

Chris crosses his ankles in front. "Well, you do. I've seen the charts. Some of you guys do, and not by much mind you. You more than them." He shrugs again. "It's such as small amount though. No one thinks that has much to do with it."

I just nod, running my toes along the seams of the tiles. "How can they find us? I mean really? Just some device picks up electro magneto brain waves or what?"

He shrugs again and toys with a thread on his pants. "Something like that. Like radio waves. At first I thought it was so super cool, but after a few years of this I realize it's kinda like how they forecast weather."

"A 'Brain Barometer'?" It's a sorry attempt at a joke, but hey, at least I tried. Chris is easy to talk to. "My son would've gotten a kick out of that." My heart seems like it has stopped beating. My kids. I have been so wrapped up in everything here I haven't really given much thought to them. "I miss him. I miss *them*."

He only grunts in understanding.

"I miss joking with them. I miss their smiles. I miss tucking them in at night. I miss dreaming with them."

"Their futures?"

"No. Never mind."

"Oh, daydreaming." He nods, a small smile on his face.

"No." Now I'm getting annoyed. It would be so nice to have someone to talk to about these things, without the fear of being gassed into submission.

He looks my way. "What do you mean?"

"I called it *dream linking*, though I don't know if there is a technical name for it. Forget it. Never mind."

"Dream linking?"

I don't bother to answer, and close my eyes. I just remember the smell of dinosaur breath. Running for my life, and those of my kids. Of being eaten, knowing I saved my kids. Of dragons, their smell and fire. The beat of their wings. I remember the swirl of energy as I faced them at compound in my dreams. I recall the night that my two munchkins were linked together in their own dream, fighting their own demons. I abruptly open my eyes.

"Do they have my kids?"

Chris gives me a funny look and changes the subject to Christmas and New Year's Eve plans here at the compound. All I really notice is he didn't answer my question.

CHAPTER 32

Derk holds my hand as we walk along the shoreline. It's been a few weeks since my massive scare and share. It has brought us closer together. He understands more than he did before. I appreciate him staying with me, not only then, but even more now. Only two people really knew all that went on with me, in my head, in my dreams.

Today is dedicated to spending some "serious quality time" as Derk announced early this morning. He has a small backpack holding our snacks and beverages that throws off his balance as we traverse this new trail. We usually take a different trail when we would walk. According to Shadow, all of us were stepping outside our comfort zones. The trail winds along with the water to our left, and sandy, rocky ledges growing underneath us and to our right as we continue. After a bit, the path narrows preventing us from holding hands. I agree to protect his pride for if, and more likely when, he'd lose his balance, and go first. We continue laughing and joking, so I don't feel it at first. By the time we come around another bend I knew it had been there awhile.

Can you hear me now?

I look back at my man shaking the sand from his shoes. My eyes were darting around trying to find the source. It was a man's voice. Quiet. Muffled. Distant. I hadn't ever heard it before. I can't see or pick up on anyone around us as I continue forward. Derk hadn't heard it, but I knew he could sense something was wrong because of my actions. My cautious movements would have alerted him if my head scanning all surroundings had not. Slowly, carefully selecting my upcoming placement of my steps, I take in more of our surroundings. The pines growing along the coast here have long needles that are waving on their thin branches with the coastal breeze coming up from the water, and then I notice their scents are missing. I can barely smell the water and sand.

"Derk?" I stop. I call for the energy. It's not there, and I don't know if I should be worried or reassured. I reach back and take his hand. "Something's not right here." My eyes meet his.

He scans the terrain like I do, and points forward, indicating he wants to keep moving. So we do. Cautiously. Stealthily. It's like it should be happening at night, and we're half expecting some wild, rabid animal or crazed person to jump out at us. After what feels like eternity, but in actuality more like ten minutes, his guard is going down. I can feel it. From his hand holding mine to the energy he's emitting. He thinks whatever it is I was sensing has passed. I'm not so sure.

Another bend and through the pines I see a building, like a factory, ahead. The path keeps heading straight for it, and I feel compelled to ask for the energy again. Again, nothing. No tingle. No warning. Nothing. Null. I scan the windows, searching for any sign of danger. Or life. Or...something.

A deep horn blows, startling me and Derk. It had come from the building. As we continue forward along the sandy path that slowly widens, I brace for attack. My adrenalin runs through me, and I grip Derk's hand more tightly. Another minute passes as we continue forward, drawn.

The doors before us open and people come out. No one pays us much mind as they joke amongst themselves.

Varying ages, but mostly adults. Some look like they are still in their teens. They all disperse, some heading right for us. I stiffen, not knowing what to expect as a small group nears us. I step off the path and Derk follows suit.

"Hi. Excuse me," says the one closest to us as he heads down the path we had just come up. Others nod and smile briefly as they pass. We watch as they all pass and head down. I watch, following them with my eyes until they are out of sight.

Derk shakes his head and chuckles. "Yep, something is wrong. Everyone else is at work."

I look around, filled with disbelief, and watch as some of the people head off toward the right side of the building. I start to follow, not quickly, just going. Derk's hand forces me to stop. "No. Stop. We're okay."

A bird chirps and I jump. I follow him back down the path, but I know have to figure out what just happened. Halfway down the path, I feel the familiar friendly energy tease my hair and clothes, and the smell of sand, surf, and pine. Comforting. Calming. But I cannot forget. Something here was important.

I carefully sit up on my cot and look around my room. I haven't been gassed. I had just dream linked with Two, and I haven't been gassed. Slowly, I rub the tired from my eyes and swing my feet to the cold floor.

What had that dream meant? No energy? Weird building? It was definitely hard seeing it all through her eyes, knowing she was anxious, almost panicking. Two is so strong and confident, so it's very hard to see her so...afraid.

But this I do know. I had heard that voice before. It was the one from my school versus bomb dream sequence.

And the path continues past the right side of the building. There it follows a hill. I already know that I have followed it dozens of times, even though it feels like the first time. No, I know it's the first time. So why do I have memories of it? I look down and see snowshoes on my feet and realize that it is snow covered this time. When did that happen? I can feel the energy, faintly leading me. The path narrows and I know, like an understanding of multiple times doing this, that I had to take off the snowshoes if I was going to continue. So I do. And I continue up, and up.

I see my objective.

Mommy?
I sit up again. My eyes frantic looking for him. I heard him. My son. But my room is empty except for me. My eyes squeeze shut. Did I imagine his voice? It had sure sounded like my Dude. Like he was right beside me. Was I really going crazy?

Looking about in the darkened room I call home, I shudder. Again I await the gas to knock me out. I have had two very vivid dreams, and yet they hadn't hit me with it yet. Were they were letting me be?

For who knows how many times this evening, I swing my feet to the cold floor. I don't want to lie back down. I don't want to dream. I want to...do anything but dream. So weird, I had just mentioned I wanted to dream link again, and all of a sudden I do.

Two? I await her response.
Nothing.

I pace my small cell and think about the building, what I had seen and felt there. I know where the path leads. What was my objective? Was it a person? A building? I couldn't remember.

After several passes around my room I hope I've worked out the urge to dream. Sometimes in the past when I've done this I don't go back into those dreams. I think I've walked and stretched for about thirty minutes, my tired and weakened muscles protesting every move. I know I'm feeling stronger, that the residual effects of my "time out" are diminishing, though I still feel angry about what they have done to me. Keeping me sedated, near comatose, had weakened my body, but not my mind.

What can they possibly think to accomplish by treating me like that? It wasn't like I was diseased. I must be a threat for some reason for talking in my dreams, or dreaming like I do. Why was it so unusual? It was all I knew.

Intimidation. A weapon.

I looked around, almost pinching my arm to ensure I wasn't asleep in some freaked out nightmare. But yet, I knew I was awake. Wide awake. And now, almost frightened.

It was him, the voice. From the school bombing sequence. *Who are you?*

They haven't told you about me? Well, let me tell you what I know.

And right then, in the early hours of morning, I learned the story of Edward.

Derk sleeps beside me, oblivious to what I have just witnessed and dreamt. I am at a loss. Did Derk and I have a hike to this place where I was so afraid, where there was no energy? Or was that my first, very own nightmare?

Ugh, now I have to wait until he wakes up.

I flop back into the sheets and fluffy pillow.

Bureau of Federal Energy and Interest   NRG-ASE

Case #: R00013ASE   Case Name: Rebecca
DOB: 07/23/1974   Code: energy

CLASSIFIED

Observation time/date: 24 December 2008/1003hrs
Report type: Weekly follow-up
Time in observation: 68 days
Weight: 148lbs
Status: conscious
Method of medication: NA

Notes:

Rebecca (Case #: R00013ASE) continues to recuperate after Roberts ordered her to be awakened due to lack of energy/activity. Subject has lessened motor skills and is still weak. Rehab has continued, x19 days.

Constant levels from the subject have been detected, but will be allowed as activity is deemed safe per agreement with subject. Energy spikes continue to be noted periodically, especially when subject is asleep, but not always in REM cycles.

Subject still refuses most conversation and activity. Subject asked Chris for writing supplies as a way to combat boredome. Roberts complied with a water-soluble marker and a limited quantity of papers. Chris is to deliver . Chris has asked subject if she wants to come to the Holly-daze Feast commencing @ 1700 hrs, and asked if Corrine can help "get her presentable." Corrine consents if it's in her quarters only. "No spying." Roberts protested, but gave in, as he will have the rooms swept to remove "dangerous contraband" prior to visit, and will return items after.

Bureau of Federal Energy and Interest

DD Form 99-ASE   BFEI-USA   Subject Record

CHAPTER 33

I need you. Shadow calls for me, and I come. There's pain in her message, and I know what time it is. The time for a lot of pain, followed by joy. Her daughter is about to make her debut.

It has been a week since that disturbing dream of the hike with my husband. He assured me we had never been to a place like that, but there were other trails yet unexplored. I had quickly assured him that that wouldn't be necessary. In that week, I have not even visited my other self. I have been too self-absorbed, and trying to mentally grasp what had happened. Both Shadow and Derk had gone round and round with reasons and "calm down" bouts.

Are you coming?

I quickly send an affirmation and then dress. Giving my sleeping hubby a quick peck, I steal into the night. My feet race with the breeze off the water.

Hank meets me at the door, so I don't even knock. The door just opens as I continue briskly in and right to my best friend's side.

She whimpers as I take her hand. "Why don't they tell you it hurts this bad?"

"I'm sure they do, all the time. It's just no one wants to listen."

"It cannot be worth this kind of pain."

"Oh, the bad stuff hasn't even happened yet."

Her eyes find mine. Hers have no humor. Mine do. "Not funny." When I chuckle she frowns. "Remind me to laugh at you when you have kids."

Another contraction, but this time I can help take some of the ache away. The energy knows about the life joining us out here soon, and helps me soothe my friend. "It'll be over soon."

"How do you know?" Her eyes glare at me.

"Because I'm me, and I do." I see Hank with the midwife between Shadow's legs. "Sure you want to wait to know what it is?"

"Don't ruin it now! We've waited nine months. I can wait a few more minutes." Her eyes go intense. "It'll be just a few more minutes right? Not like...hours or something?"

Another contraction makes her groan, but the rest of us in the room chuckle.

The midwife starts giving more direction, and Hank tries to figure out if he wants to hold Shadow's hand, or watch for the baby's departure from the womb. Back and forth he goes between her hands and asking the midwife what he can do, all the while Shadow mutters warnings about "Pick a spot already!" and "Don't make me smack you!"

The door opens and shuts hurriedly, and the draft is welcome. I hadn't realized how warm it had become in here. I don't even look to see who it is. "Did I wake you?"

Derk sits on the other side of Shadow's abdomen. "Nope. But when I got cold, and you were gone, I remembered you telling me it was going to be tonight."

Shadow hisses with another contraction, then thanks my husband for making Hank's decision more easy. Derk picks up her left hand, while I continue to hold her right.

The midwife asks the guys to help hold Shadow's legs; that the baby's coming.

"I can see the head crowning!" Poor Hank cries.

I have waited over nine months to tell her this, "It's

a girl!"

"Dammit!" she hisses. "I'm still pushing!" Another contraction. "You couldn't wait for five more minutes?"

"Sorry." I cringe knowing I let the cat out of the bag. "Maybe it's a boy?" But I can see the smile on her face. She's about to be the proud mommy of a princess.

About thirty minutes later, a warm bundle rests at her breast, and her husband at her side. Shadow's smile and coos fill the room where crying and sounds of pain had just been.

That is how is should be, I think.

The midwife softly speaks about what to look for, reminding them how to change and bathe their new bundle, that they shouldn't be quiet or the baby would never be able to sleep with noise going on. She continues on with feeding schedules, making sure the baby gets a good latch, and a myriad of other things. I mentally catalogue these notes just in case I ever get the gumption to become a mom.

Derk just holds me close as we cuddle on the sofa until he notices Hank's head do a bob. Gently he pries away long enough to stand and do an exaggerated stretch, "Weeelll...ah! Time to get going so you all can get some rest." He offers me a quick wink. "Bedtime? Round two?"

"With an invitation like that?" My sarcasm is pretty heavy. "Absolutely."

Our walk home is longer than the trip to Hank and Shadow's place since the urgency is gone. He holds my hand as we walk in the still evening breeze.

"You had to spill the beans, didn't you?" It was soft, and laced with humor.

"I was excited," I counter.

"You, my dear, were early. And you claim to see the future or something."

He receives a mock slug as I tease back, "I know what's in your future if you keep picking on me." At his raised eyebrows, "The couch." And I take off towards the house a full two seconds ahead of him, laughing as I go.

    Carefully I sit upright. My sleep drugged eyes find the small clock Chris has slipped into my room. The hands read almost three thirty. I note that our time seems to be in the same zone for a change, versus her days to my nights.

    Shadow Danza, or whatever her last name is now, is a mommy. I feel both happy and lost. I miss mine, and wonder where they are. If they were on the run. Would they have chosen Alaska? Hawaii? Texas? Maine? Or if they were still in Stevens Point, or somewhere close by.

    Sleep holds no welcome for me now. Sitting on the cold floor, I start my stretches and exercises that Chris has had me doing for the past few months. Bitterness taints any good they do.

CHAPTER 34

Chris has become my constant companion, and I find myself opening up to him. Though he's a big burly man, I have felt his compassion. Not only when I was coming out of the drugged coma the agency had enforced upon me, and my messy reentry into consciousness, nor the way he fills the chair in my room to prevent my boredom after "outings" to see the government and medical staff. It's in the way he meets my eyes, not in fear, but...compassion, like he gets what I feel and doesn't think I'm this awful threat to the way of American life or defense. He's calm and confident, and I think he does that stupid tapping of the syringe when we are on the "outings" out of boredom and to tell the others in the rooms and halls that it's there, but...maybe I'm projecting, "How silly all this is."

I look at my script and the pages before me. Chris had not questioned my wanting some paper to keep my sanity. Interesting enough he had almost warned me not to write anything incriminating. Knowing I better not put that in my writings, I also wonder if he could be one of the few people that Jay had told me lingered and still offered information about the agency when I had been hiding in Stevens Point, Wisconsin.

Sighing, I continue.

> I'm grateful for the simple gift of the Crayola washable marker in black, and the small stack of loose white sheets of paper.
>
> I wonder how long I have actually been here. I know Chris and some of the staff mentioned the holidays, but I haven't really seen any decorations or heard any Christmas Carols filling the air. Chris did tell me a few weeks or so ago about some of the plans people had, but I was sure I wouldn't be able to participate in any festivities.
>
> Uhm,...what else to write.
>
> It's been about 2 weeks since the dream about SD having a baby. A few nights ago I remember waking with the memory of holding her small bundle. I could smell the new baby smell I almost remember from my kids. I haven't dreamt since that.
>
> I wonder if I should write my dreams down. Journal them or something. Maybe that would be "beneficial" for them, and maybe then I would be

able to see what they find so interesting about my "ability."

It still makes me sick. I didn't choose to dream this other place, another version of me, the understanding of the energy there and in some of my other dreams.

I miss my kids. I swear I hear them from time to time. I know I'm probably suffering from some sort of delusions, or just maybe remembering the sound of their voices. I remember brushing my daughter's hair and her pulling away when I'd come across a nest of tangles. She'd pull away like I had tried to hurt her on purpose. Like a mom would do that. I might not have been the girliest of moms, but I loved the way she would try out some hairdos on me.

I remember 20+ twirly-ma-bobs and little kid barrettes all tangled in my hair and her being so proud at her 3yr old mind's creation.

Smiling I remember the whole of that day. It must have taken her all of half-an-hour to use every hair thingy we had.

"Mommy's so preddy."

"Yes, I am pretty," I had said, secretly wondering how on earth I was going to be able to get all those little clips and things out without going bald. "You did a great job! You should always do my hair."

She had beamed at that.

I remember I had left those things in my hair for a couple hours, including their bath time and then they were off to bed. It took me over an hour to get what I could out. I found a few more when I showered that night. I had a few more greet me in the morning when I tried to brush my hair.

"That must have been a sight," his heavy drawl lets me know he's in my room.

Without looking up, "I was gorgeous." I shoot him a look at his deep chuckle. "You don't knock anymore." I look back at my paper and try to straighten the pages into a neat little stack.

"Do I have to?" Again, a slight teasing tone. I know he's hinting at nothing is private concerning me.

"Might be nice," I huff. "I used to have a sign above my door to my kitchen that said, 'No one gets in to see the Wizard. Not no one. Not no how.' *Wizard of Oz*," I smile, just for a moment. Standing I look at him, "Need something?"

"Wizard?"

"What?" I feel the taunt in my voice as I say it.

Chris just shakes his head as he chuckles some more. "Any-who, small get together in our cafeteria, and I got permission to bring you."

My brows furrow as I ask, "'Get together'?"

Chris opens the door to my dungeon and holds his arm out indicating I'm to pass through, "Christmas Eve meal."

"It's Christmas Eve?" My voice sounds so quiet, like a whisper.

It's my first Christmas Eve without my babies. The sadness of that hits hard and quick, and I try not to cry. No Christmas tree filled with shining lights and bulbs resting atop colorful packages. No presents at all. None from me, nor for me.

"Yep," his voice had been soft. "Come on, or the Twins will have eaten all the cranberries and dessert."

"I've never met them," I mutter.

"Well, no time like the present."

Slowly, I force my feet to the door. "How do I look?"

Chris takes a moment to look me over. I know he sees my worn pajamas and hospital style robe and socks. "Don't worry. We have a stop to make, and you can meet one of the twins there." Gently he takes my elbow and pushes me the direction we need to go. I keep trying to run my fingers through my limp, lanky hair to give it some sense of being ready for a public appearance. "Calm down. I wouldn't let you meet the others looking like this." At a door he stops and knocks.

"Oh, you do knock!" I try to tease despite feeling so self-conscious.

Chris just raises that darn eyebrow and waits expectantly for the door to open.

A smile was what I notice when the door opens. It takes a moment to realize it was for me, genuine and filling the hazel eyes looking at me. "So, you must be Rebecca?" The sentence ended in a question, but the tone made it clear I wasn't needing to answer. "Thanks, Chris. Anything else?" She was looking at my bodyguard, who seems unsure if he should come in with me as she was pulling me through the door.

"You've got no more than twenty minutes Corrine," he says, then he gives me a funny look. I am left wondering what it means because he turns and she shuts the door at the same time.

Nervously I run my fingers through my hair again and keep my gaze down. Seeing my robe was open on my right side, I quickly right it and tied it shut.

"My name is Corrine Casten," she is trying to get me to look up, but I only see her outstretched hand. I shake it, and drop mine again. "I bet he didn't tell you what you're doing here?" Again, a question, but more of a statement. "Well, this isn't going as I had hoped."

I look up then, not wanting to seem rude or defiant. "I'm sorry. I don't know why I'm here."

Corrine offers another smile, though not as large this time I note. "Chris asked me to let you have a shower and borrow some clothes." At my confused look she continues and now starts bustling around her space. "I guess he thinks we're about the same size."

I gasp as I watch her move away. Her space is more like a beautiful hotel suite. She has a small kitchenette with homey farm scene towels and a spice rack. A rooster and hen salt and pepper sit on the small counter by her oven. A microwave and refrigerator also fill the open space kitchenette. It's clean, but I know it's been used. "You have a kitchen?" My eyes see wine glasses in the glass front cupboards.

"Yep," she looks back at me. "And a shower." My eyes look around uncertainly, then to her arms motioning. "Come on, Rebecca. Hot, secure, and *private* shower this way."

My feet move of their own accord.

I like her.

Me too. A smile comes easy to my features knowing Two is here.

Nope, just checking in. Gotta go. Shadow needs me.

A phone rings and I jump. Corrine moves swiftly to it. "Hello?" She listens half a moment, then looks at me. "Yes." She frowns. "No." She huffs, "Oh, give me a break. Relax!" And she slams the phone down, and walks back over to me. "We're not going to have any...problems...right?"

My head shakes in the negative quickly.

"Good, come on then. You're wasting valuable time." She pulls me along. "When Chris says twenty minutes, he really means twenty, minus thirty seconds." She offers a small smile again, "Your shower awaits." She drags me through her living room equivalent and towards her bathroom, which I notice is attached to her bedroom as well. Two big plush towels are resting on the vanity and I touch them, tenderly.

My reflection shocks me. I know I had been weakened, given no showers, razorblades, or combs or brushes, but that view of myself makes me both really sick and really upset. I look away in disgust. Corrine shakes her head and adds stubbornly, "Hurry." And she shuts the door. From the other side she adds, "I'll have clothes for you when you're done."

I realize with that shutting of the door I am finally given some privacy, like she said. My first ever since I have arrived here. I quickly move to the shower and turn it on, as warm as I can stand, and watch the steam start its wafting as I strip down. I step into the river spouting out of the best showerhead I've ever been under. A sigh of pleasure escapes my lips, and I take a full minute to enjoy the feel. Looking around I quickly grab the shampoo and lather up. Another sigh of happiness escapes at the fragrance combined with warmth, and I dread coming out. After I apply some conditioner I look for a razor to shave, and find an empty razor holder.

Darn. Would've been nice.

Knowing I will need to hurry this up so I can put on some clothes and brush out my hair, I quickly rinse my hair out, and wring it to get the excess water out. The towel I grab is a full shower towel, and I cannot believe I've never owned one. Wiping down as fast as I can, I wrap it back around me, and crack open the bathroom door to see if I can spot my gracious host.

She's sitting in a comfy looking sofa reading, and looks up. "All clean?" At my nod she sets the book down and gets up. She grabs a small stack of clothes resting on the coffee table and hands them to me. "Chris is wrong. You're taller and thinner, but hopefully these are close enough."

Thanking her I take the clothes and shut the door as she steps back. On top is a simple brush to use, a travel-size toothbrush, with travel-size toothpaste, and travel-size deodorant, and I set those items on the vanity. With a slight laugh, I apply the deodorant and quickly pull on the borrowed light gray leggings, a gray cami top, and the oversized navy jersey top. Seeing the brush, I being to take on my terrible tangles.

"Five minutes!" Corrine carols through the door.

Snatching the toothbrush, I put a dollop of toothpaste on it and wet it. I scrubbed my mouth grateful for the cleaning before I have to meet people and talk more to my hostess.

"Three minutes!" Corrine calls again. "Hurry! And leave the stuff. I'll get it later! Cranberries are calling my name and I'm gonna kick my brother's bum if he doesn't leave us some."

I rinse out the toothbrush and brave a glance at the mirror again. "Better," I mumble and open the door. I look down as I come out, so I don't have to see any disappointment. "Thank you. That was wonderful."

"Well, you're welcome." At her smile, "Merry Christmas!"

"Merry Christmas," I weakly offer.

A rap at the door has Corrine rolling her eyes, followed by a loud, "We still have two minutes!" But she was already grabbing my hand and pulling me to the door. She slipped her feet into some black slippers with red berries and green holly leaves on them. "Here," and she points to a pair of cheap navy flip flops. After slipping them on, Corrine opened the door to a frowning Chris. "What? We still have a minute on *your* watch, Scrooge."

"Your brother heard the twenty minutes, and left three minutes ago."

"What! That turd!" Corrine pulls her door shut and hurries down the hall leaving us watching her disappearing around a corridor.

"Feel better?" Chris asks, eyebrow raised.

"Much; thank you for that." I mean every letter and wring my hands ahead of me.

"Good. We'll we better get going," and he starts walking in the direction Corrine all had but run, "I wasn't kidding about Caleb. Nigel told me he had seen him go."

At the corridor, I followed Chris' lead, and a few

more hallways later, the smell of food fills my nose and saliva fills my mouth. Upon making the final turn, the sight of the buffet room stops me in my tracks. There were about forty people going through and sitting around the huge room I believe to be a cafeteria. The buffet, though large, about thirty feet worth of food, wasn't what stops me. It wasn't the people eating. It was all of it, mixed with the smiles and laughing, and a real Blue Spruce Christmas tree decked out, presents and all, and that scent of Christmas Cheer.

"Merry Christmas," Chris softly offers and leads me the rest of the way to the beginning of what promises to be a fabulous meal.

CHAPTER 35

I feel confused.
1) I know someone read my last journaling. I am certain it happened either while I was at Corrine's for that awesome shower (if that's the case, now I'm not so grateful), or while I was at the (I think they called it Holly-daze something) Christmas meal. I'm leaning towards the latter as I didn't see Roberts there at all. Chris had told me that pretty much the whole compound/agency was there for that meal. I have to admit it was very good. I ate until it hurt, which unfortunately wasn't a lot.
2) Chris never left my side until we got back to my "cell." He was pleasant and tried to introduce me to others. I'm going to call them inmates. But Corrine seemed so darn nice, I feel bad in doing so. Aaron and Trevor were there visiting. They kept

a leery eye on me, that's for sure. Some even tried to start conversations with me...like they knew me. That was uncomfortable to say the least. Chris said he hadn't taken me for a hermit. Am I one? Or have I been turned into one?

3) When we left, I asked for more of a tour of the building. Chris seemed...nervous? Uncertain? Am I paranoid? Yeah, I know...he works for the enemy. But...anyway...as we walked down this hallway, I swear I felt...something?

It was me.
I pause, glancing around the simple cell I am forced to call home. It's a voice, much like the other I heard...maybe the same one.
You heard me, right?

Yes.
Definitely something. I wonder what it meant? Or if I'm reading too much into what I thought I felt?

I could feel you, too. And him.
I pretend to work out a writing cramp. Merry Christmas, Edward.
I need you to free me.
I can't. I don't have that freedom.
Help me die then.
What?! NO! My eyes fill with tears at the thought of me helping him, anyone, die. No.
This isn't living. This is a lie.
How can you even-? I stop that thought. I do

know. He's shared his story with me. He was trapped, still in my cocoon from two years ago, but more so by the agency and its fear of him. *I can't.*

You need to come see me. Then you decide.

Shaking my head, I look around, knowing someone is probably watching me. *I can't get out of here. Chris lets me out once and awhile, but I don't have free reign.*

There is a pause. A long, pregnant pause. The kind I never understood when reading about them in books. But this is one. My head starts getting fuzzy, and I realize I had been holding my breath.

Go to sleep, and come visit me. Dream of me.

The marker's cap snaps into place, and I set it on top of today's sheet of paper. I can't really answer him. Nor can I deny him. He had been through so much pain and anguish…and deceit. I understand. I empathize. I had to try to free him, one way or another.

With a sigh, I crawl into my blankets on my cot. I thought again of all the luxuries Corrine had in her suite compared to my cell-like domicile. Then I think of all the hardships Edward has faced, and I close my eyes as I turn on my side, and pull my blanket up to my ears.

I awaken.

Somehow I felt light, though my eyelids feel heavy. Tenderly I touch them and realize I can see my fingers touching my eyelids. This kind of thing has happened to me in the past, I remember, but it always seems like a surprise and fills me with awe. Carefully, I sit upright. Something feels a little different. I still feel light and aware, just too light. I look back at the cot, like I forgot something, and am startled to see myself lying there asleep, blanket up to my ears.

This is one of those astro-dream thingies I've heard and read about, I am certain. But the draw to move is stronger than my desire to figure out how it is possible. And the draw pulls me, not towards my cell's door, but towards the two-way mirror, and then through it.

My first glimpse of what is really behind that "mirror" gives me pause. A uniformed lady sits monitoring a computer screen that is showing a "blip" of some sort as she's tapping the screen. Her name tag says Johnston. Her fingers type away some message as she looks at my prone figure in the cot, blankets to my ears, and back to the "blip" screen. Computers are everywhere, monitoring air temperature, documenting when I sleep, positions I sleep in, and other stuff. But the big button by the window beckons, and I take a closer look. The energy tells me what the name validates, PANIC.

This way.

It's that same hill, going through the pines and snow, just past the factory. I know where I need to go, and I look around. Seems like the trees represent a cement hallway, like a memory.

This way.

I know that voice. That's not from here. It's from *her* place. It's pulling me, and her, to the top of this path. I know there's a cabin there, and I remember getting to the door, and it opening. Then that's all. Like that was it. I know I need to get going.

This is important.

The hallway reminds me of trees as I negotiate them in the near darkness. I have a sense of déja vu, again, for the umpteenth time in my life. But I press on, and then I see it. The hallway Chris and I had been in when I had felt that odd sensation.

Me.

You.

My astro form continues down the hallway, but I know something is wrong. The signal is weak. *I missed it.* So I go back the way I had come. *Stronger...and then not so much.* And again I have to backtrack. And yet again I move to where I feel the energy telling me I have to be.

And stop.
      Before me and behind me is the hallway I have gone down. One either side is the cement walls with reinforcements jutting out every six feet or so. It almost does look like tree trunks with the eerie cast off lights indicating corridors and exits. But where is the entrance to where Edward is?

      I can see the door.
      It's a part of the cabin.
      I turn the knob.
      It doesn't budge.
      Why can't I open it?

      I feel Two and can almost see her vision lying over the top of mine.
      Of course they wouldn't want me to see his door. They would want to protect him, from others, well as me. It's like a mirage. It is to my left, in a more central location to the compound. Thoughts of dragons and my compound fight for control of my dream flash before me, but I struggle to keep my connection with Edward.
      And pass through the cement trees.

      A cocoon of energy blinds me as I cross through the door's threshold. It's so brilliant I have to blink to let my eyes adjust. Cautiously, I approach it. My skin tingles being near it, like goose bumps. My hand reaches to touch the cocoon, and it changes color.
      A red light goes off in the corner of the room.
      Hurry. They know someone's here.
      His voice comes from within the cocoon, and I reach in, unafraid and confident.
      It's hard to explain all of what happens next, but this is what I know.
      The cocoon dissolves revealing a poor corpse of a form, linked to a few dozen tubes and wires. A sheet lay

draped across it, and I step up closer to the form.

Free me. All the way.

I will not kill you. Nor can I let you die. My hands reach out again, this time gently lifting the sheet to find where all the wires and tubes went. A poor limp hand linked to a limp arm greet my sorry eyes. Carefully, I grasp what I can of his hand.

Pain and misery overwhelm my senses, and I let go. After a half second I regrip the hand and allow the energy that has been missing from the room to flow through me.

The form sighs, a gurglish sound, and I look towards the grotesque face. Eye crusties cake the closed lids, and I wish to ease them away.

What are you doing? I told you to kill me. The voice seems angry, confused.

But you are not supposed to die. I don't get to choose. The energy does.

But they are coming!

I know.

The energy is weakening me as it floods into Edward's prone figure. His skin changes from a pasty white to a light pink. And I know I need to turn off his sedation. The IV in his arm glows for just a second, and I know that that's the one keeping him down. I stop the flow with a thought, my eyes tightly closed with the effort to give him life from my already weakened energy.

Once you wake, Edward, be calm. Don't fight them. They don't want to hurt you for fear of the end of days. I have to go.

With that thought I feel myself slipping into the hallway where people are starting to congregate, some with Tasers and other weapons. Chris stands half-awake, with a syringe at the ready. The sight of this gives me pause. Slowly, he turns my direction, like he can feel me, or see me.

"Chris?" a male nurse asks him. "You ready?'

Chris shakes his head. "Yeah. Hopefully Edward's in a good mood." With a final glance in my direction he faces the door, and waits like everyone else.

I slide more and more, passing the now standing Johnston who's with a very irate Roberts. Quickly, I glide back into my cot, under my blanket, pulled up to my ears.

I stand beside Edward as he begins to gain consciousness here in the little room in the cabin. The energy holds him now, and it's cautious. I know what happened in *her* world, only through what's happening in mine.

We are rescuing Edward.

The memories of what he's told her of his abilities and experiences make me leery of his intentions. As do the recollections of him asking to die, or for her to kill him. No doubt, he was in a bad condition, but the cocoon must have helped him some over the past two years or so.

Where I was I could understand now why there was no energy, and why I had felt so weird that day with Derk so many weeks ago. It was Edward in a cocoon, with the agency. And now, he was indeed free.

His eyes open weakly. "You're still here?" His voice sounds like a toad croaking.

"We are." I answer back.

He smiles weakly, and goes back to sleep.

"Don't worry," I offer as I stand a little closer. "We've got you."

I can feel the commotion outside his room at the compound as if it was right outside the cabin. I knew it would only be a matter of time until they got brave enough to open the door and see what was and wasn't there for them.

I cannot help but smile.

CHAPTER 36

Captain Roberts stands and stares at the empty bed, sans all the wires and tubes. He had yet to close the wide open trap most call a mouth. Chris stands beside him, as do nine others of the best there at the compound. "Search the grounds," he whispers. When no one moved, he barks, "Search the grounds!"

Chris takes a step back and eyes the others in the room. "No one is that stupid, Roberts. No one is going to take on Edward, especially if he can just pass through walls."

Roberts never turns. "How'd he get out?"

One of the nurses chirps up, "Never passed us."

Chris agrees, and asks, "What took you so long?"

Roberts doesn't make eye contact, "You know where I was. Watching her spike like no other."

Chris looks at the hidden door, then back to the floor.

Roberts looks at the security camera in the corner by the still red flashing light. "I want to see those tapes. Now! Chris, come with me. The rest of you, clean up this mess and keep your eyes and ears alert!"

Chris falls in step with Roberts all the way down to the central security room, where all the monitors' findings are recorded. Roberts takes out a key and opens the door and Chris follows inside the small room. Quickly Roberts finds the monitor he's looking for and hits rewind to go back to when Edward's form was in the cocoon just fifteen to twenty minutes before. He puts the images on a bigger screen, like he has with Rebecca's, and hits play.

At first there's nothing.

Then, just before the red light starts flashing, there's a shimmer, very faint at the side of Edward's bed. It lingers for a moment, then the cocoon brightens and all but dissolves right there on film. Roberts gasps in shock. "What the-"

Chris keeps his eyes on the screen and the slight shimmer.

The shimmer seems to move and expand, for just a moment, no more than five seconds, and then Edward is gone. All that was left is the wires and various tubes and needles left behind. He had just disappeared…and so did the shimmer.

Chris keeps his eyes on the screen, even after Roberts hits stop, rewinds, and plays it again. Roberts doesn't say a word this time. He just watches it. The whole thing lasts less than a minute. And Roberts wants to memorize each precious second.

Roberts mutters, "It had to be her."

Chris looks over and raises his brow in a question.

"What? You asked me where I was. I was with Johnston who had just reported a weird…anomaly…a spike." Roberts rubs his hands across his face. "I was watching her in her little bed…with her little blanket pulled up to her ears…spiking. Then, warning lights and bells and whistles-"

"Bells and whistles?" Chris raises his eyebrow even higher.

"-and then a cold, shiver runs through me…and her spike is over." Roberts points to the little screen showing Rebecca sleeping away.

"A shiver?" Chris clears his throat. "Really? I get that you're freaked out by her and her dreams and energy spikes, but she never left her bed." Chris points to the little monitor, "And there she sleeps. Oooooh, I'm shaking in my bedtime slippers."

Roberts scowls at the burly man. "I felt a chill, a shiver."

Chris can't help himself, "I got chills, they're multiplyin', and I'm losin' control-"

Roberts stops the video. "Not funny. We're missing one very powerful, very dangerous, angry...subject."

"And why would he be so angry?" Chris pokes.

"Shut up. This isn't some joke. He's gone! And she-" he points to the monitor showing a now turning-in-her-sleep Rebecca "-had something to do with it."

"And where did she put him, when she didn't leave her room? Under her bed like the boogie man?" Chris jibs again.

"I don't know." Roberts admits, "But I'm gonna find out."

Chris straightens, "Well, on a good note...the world didn't end."

CHAPTER 37

"It was you, wasn't it? In the hallway?"
Chris is taking me to my next "session" with Roberts and his medical, psychological entourage. He had come into my cell with a weird look, and explained that I had a meeting to go to this morning. He had waited quietly in his chair as I brushed my teeth and tried to brush some of the tangles out of my hair. He had been quiet all the way until we left my room.
I pause, "Me? When? What hallway?"
Chris looks down both ends of the hallway we're in. "I felt you. Like when you're in your cell and I'm in that uncomfortable chair. Like when you're writing and I'm looking over your shoulder to see what you've written about me."
"I don't write anything...much...about you." My eyes can't make his face, so I know he knows I'm lying. I reflect a moment on his words as we stand there in silence. "You felt me?"
Chris nods and starts us off in the direction of my "session" once again. "Yeah...you're an energy chick, remember?" After a couple of steps, "So that's a confession?"
I half stumble, "No. I wanted...clarification...as to

what you meant. Like...uhm...you 'felt' I had been at fault versus...'feeling me.' That's what I meant." I look straight forward as we continue. "No confession. I haven't done anything wrong."

After a few more steps, "What is it that I've supposedly done?"

Chris slants me a look, and after a few more steps, "Helped somebody."

I reflect a moment, "That sounds like something I'd do...help somebody." I see the door before us. "So, am I being congratulated?"

Chris shakes his head, "Nope." He knocks on the door, and then opens it, motioning me to go inside.

Roberts waits with his usual groupies, but they look tired. Very tired. And today, there's a television and DVD player in the room with us. I take all this in quickly before I go to my usual chair and Chris to his. Before Roberts are pictures and notes and some computer sheets. His eyes have followed me as I came in and they bore into my skull now as I look down.

"Why are you looking down, Rebecca?" Roberts asks sweetly, too sweetly. "Have a guilty conscious?"

"Leading the witness," Chris chirps.

I look between the men, and beg for an innocent face, "Guilty conscious? For what?" I note Chris won't meet my glances, but Roberts definitely does.

Roberts stands, "I thought you said you deserved respect. That you hadn't given us reason to distrust you."

I meet his look firmly, "That's right."

His eyes, like heat seekers, "Is that still true?"

I blink, and pray it looks innocent. "Yes." My voice sounds so soft, not very convincing, even to my own ears.

Roberts notices and shakes his head, "Thought we had an understanding."

"We do. I'm not doing anything." I am honest in that, because at that moment I don't even feel Two. "I don't want trouble. And I don't want to be comatose all the time like-"

Roberts eyes still bore into me, "Like who?"

"Like...how you had me before." I know I'm scrambling, but I can't lie. I don't ever want to fail a lie detector, or have that on my conscience. "Being alive via tubes and wasting away because you have me sedated."

Roberts narrows his eyes and takes me in. I glance at the others at the table, and realize that I am their sole focus. No pens and paper, no scribbling today. I glance as Chris who just taps that damn syringe, and I realize I hadn't noticed it before. When Roberts moves, my gaze flies to him. He moves to the television and presses play on the machine hooked up to it. My eyes immediately recognize the room and the cocoon on the screen. Quickly I mask my feelings, and watch the quick five minutes he shows everyone.

When it's over I ask, "What is this?"

Roberts hits stop, rewind, stop again, play, then pause, then slow forward, so it's like screen by painful screen showing what had happened to the occupant of that room. I sit mesmerized by the slight shimmer within the room and seeming to move to the bed holding a corpse draped in a sheet, and the faint flare-up of the cocoon before it disappears. There is movement of the sheet and the obvious shimmer around the prone figure's hand, then to his face. Then, a swirl, and he was gone. The prone figure had vanished. And the shimmer retreated. Roberts hit pause just before the shimmer fully left the screen.

I blink in surprise.

It looks like a face.

I know it is my face. I can't lie about it, but I'd have to come up with something if they guessed it to be me. I don't know what Roberts would do to me, but all sorts of thoughts flooded my mind in that instant.

"I was watching you *sleep* last night," Roberts twists out. It made me want to scream at the indecency of it. "I was called in to see you when you...had an episode." His eyes dare to call me a liar.

I swallow, trying to compose myself. "You watched me have an episode...one of my dreams?"

Roberts leaves the image of the partial shimmery face on the screen and takes his seat. "That's you, isn't it?"

I look back to the screen, then back to him. "I don't know what you want me to say," I answer honestly.

"I want you to tell me how you did it," he begins. "And second, where is Edward?"

I can feel everyone's eyes on me. I know this for certain, I'm in trouble. I have no idea how to answer this without perjuring myself terribly. After a few seconds, "I don't know where...Edward...is."

The rest of the "session" goes by in a blur, with that damn television showing that face, my face, the whole time. I feel numb. I realize with that last statement, I really didn't know where Edward was. I am also very aware that Two hasn't been here to offer her support. I don't know where that left me with Roberts, or anyone else in that room. Nor do I recall how long that interrogation actually was.

As we head back to my cell, Chris keeps silent all the way up to the final turn before my door. Then he pushes me up against the cement wall of the hallway, but not roughly, just...forcibly. "How?"

I just look into his frowning face. I can see he is concerned, but I don't know it it's for Edward, his job, or me. "I don't know."

He just looks at me, and time seems to stop. The energy calls to me, and I follow its call.

I see a man's back as he walks away. But I know that back. I know that walk. I know that hair. It is familiar and then again, not. I thought it was gone from me forever, and into the arms of another. Hope surges within me.

"Rebecca?"

I hear Chris' voice, but I cannot tear my eyes from the form making a left turn down a corridor. "Chase?" I take a step towards the corridor, but Chris' bulk prevents further passage.

"What?" he questions.

I look into his face, then back down the hall. "Is my husband here?"

Chris gives me a weird look, mutters to himself, and leads me to my cell's door. Once I'm inside I cannot shake the feeling that that was indeed Chase. As Chris turns to leave, I reach out for his arm. "Chris, was that my husband? Are my children here?"

Chris looks me square in the eye, "No."

With that I collapse on my cot, gripping my blanket.

And he leaves, locking the door once again behind him.

CHAPTER 38

I sit with the paper and marker in my hand ready to write all that I feel. Yet I know my written thoughts are readable, and hence dangerous. So I just sit, poised to write. Instead I just think it all out.

First, I know as sure as there is a sun and a moon, that I had seen Chase earlier. I also know that I had screwed up in asking Chris if it had been him. There went any chance for escape for sure. Now Chris would have others on watch, so any chance of escape would be hindered.

Second, that I was not crazy thinking I had heard my son however many days ago it had been.

Third, that somehow the energy had transported Edward...somewhere.

Fourth, that Two wasn't talking to me anymore.
Well, that's a bit harsh.
I drop my marker. Smiling, I pick it back up. She hadn't left me. *Where have you been?* I feel bad for chastising her, but I need to let her know how utterly alone I have been.
Taking care of Edward. He's quite the character.
I listen as she fills me in on all that has gone on in her life. She tells me how shocked she was about the cabin and Edward's tie there, more so with his being able to cross

to where she was. Neither of us understand it. But both of us talk about how we had each felt the energy do what it did. I explain the trouble it had caused here with them distrusting me.

Well, they can't distrust you that much. They didn't gas you when I joined you.

I acknowledge her being right on that subject, but tell her of my fear of them doing that to me again.

Don't worry. Maybe I can bring you here.

My whole body tenses. *What?*

Like we did with Edward?

But we didn't do that. The energy did. Maybe Edward helped. I mentally shake that off. *Change of subject.*

I mention Chris saying he had known it was me in the hall that night. Tell her that he had "felt" me. We discuss all the meanings behind that at great length. Two seems to believe maybe Chris as a mole, or that he has some abilities as well. And here I was hoping it just meant he understood me, that he got me.

I also mention my sighting of Chase. She only listens. Then I ask her if she knew anything concerning my kids.

Nope. They haven't come a visiting lately. Guess I hadn't been looking for them. Been kinda busy with Shadow and the lil one.

Shadow's baby girl has been doing well. I hadn't realized that they had named her Rebecca Jo for me and my daughter. That kind of tribute meant more than I could say. She said she'd pass on my gratitude and well wishes for me.

A yawn passed my lips...and she knew.

It's still early. Are you really tired, or am I boring you?

No, I admit. *I guess I'm still tired from the Edward thing.*

She said she understood, and that she'd visit me soon. I wasn't really listening. I was already falling asleep. Falling....

Guess they...

        gassed...   me...

                      after all.

    Chris stands by Roberts. "Okay, she's out. Let it go." And Chris is on the move, and out the door.
    Roberts lifts his hand from the PANIC button. But his eyes don't leave her form as it sways, passed out, sheets of paper falling from her hands. Her body tries to right itself, still in a sitting position where it has succumbed to the airborne sedative released just moments before. Roberts isn't worried as Chris unlocks the door. Roberts just has his hand at the ready over that simple little button.
    Chris quickly enters her room and grasps her form, bringing it into a laying pose, and left, secures the door behind him. Within seconds, he is huffing beside Roberts again. "There, she's all settled in then."
    Roberts looks at Chris. "You care for her?"
    Chris raises his eyebrow. "What's that supposed to mean?"
    Roberts continues to give Chris a cold look. "She's not to be trusted."
    Chris shakes his head and walks out. "And you are?"

    I stay with her through the night, knowing only the energy between us can protect her should she come into trouble.
    After a few hours, something quiet startles me. It was so soft and faint. Straining, I listen.
    Mommy?
    I smile and draw on the energy to give her this. She needs this one dream with her kids. They had come a calling.

CHAPTER 39

Edward joins Derk and me on the beach as the sun sets. This has been our ritual for the past two years. Ever since he had been transported here, I told him of the water and our, mine and my other's, to it. And since then, the water moves weird, rather like it did when I knew she had been drugged and trapped by the agency she had willingly gone to. Since, the water has done that slow rise and fall, like someone in deep slumber. I know it's her.

No energy flows here. No gulls fill the lack-luster sky. This beach is a now and has been a mirror of her sedated state. It almost hurts to be here every day. But we come, every day. We, the silent monitors and saddened friends of our comatose comrade.

I know Edward feels guilty. Feels guilty for her having to take this punishment and abuse for his freedom. His body's stance still speaks the volume of his inner turmoil.

For the first few months, Edward's anger and strong urge to get back and fight all but consumed him. Then came the sullen state of depression. The long days in isolation and long nights awake, staring out into nothingness, were how he had spent his time.

Derk insisted on befriending Edward, then showed him around. The cabin up past the factory had in actuality been abandoned and left for ruin. But for two men, it became a bonding place as they fixed it back up into a passable domicile for Edward to live in. Though none of us knew for how long. But for nearly two years Edward had called that home, and us "friends."

And during the past couple of years, Edward had showed me some of his "abilities" and I had showed him ours. As I had seen him "strut his stuff," I remember thinking, *That's it? That's what had them so worked up?* But I never shared those thoughts, not even to Shadow.

Shadow stayed clear of him, fearing for her now walking and talking Rebecca Jo. But I have seen her from time to time, watching us all as we stand in the sand of the beach, and wonder if she would come down this time. But she never had. In order to spend time with her, it was an unspoken rule, "No Edward." And, I miss her. Wanted to share what I knew of him. Want her to open up to him. But, I respect her wishes, and visit without Edward, with no mention of Edward, or what Edward said or did. It was like he wasn't as big of a deal in my life as he was.

Looking back I see her. She's standing back by the trees. I can tell she's watching the still bizarre way the water is moving and has since shortly after Edward arrived, and I lost my connection to her. When he arrived, I feel like I lost both my other self and Shadow, and I wonder if she thinks that way too.

Please Shadow. I'm not sure she'll listen, or even let me in enough to hear me. She hasn't given me any indication she's heard me for a long time. *Please. She needs us. All of us. And I cannot live like this without you. We've been friends for far too long.* It's the same mental plea mantra I've been saying for the past few months, when I've seen her out like this, watching the waves. Usually after that, she leaves, never looking at me or Derk, or Edward.

    Her shoulders sag.
    My heart hopes.
    Derk squeezes my hand.
    My hope dies.

Eyes find mine. But they are not hers. They are Edward's, as he has come to stand a little closer to me. Then his find her, standing alone by those almost masking pines. "She still comes to watch it with us."

I nod. "But she won't join me. Not like she used to." I look back up to her figure. No wind to toy with her hair, though she keeps it shorter now because of her daughter. "I keep hoping she will come around."

Edward's eyes stay on Shadow. Then he starts walking directly towards her.

"No!" I call, half-heartedly. Part of me knows he has to do this. The other part wonders if she'll even let him.

But as is now common for Edward, he does as he pleases, and keeps going. His strides aren't overly confident, but they don't slow. His approach does not go unnoticed. Shadow's eyes have left the waves' sad excuse for cresting, and stare down the man heading her way. She doesn't move away. She doesn't move anything but her head as she watches him near.

Derk again squeezes my hand, and pulls me along, following the footsteps recently left in the sand. "Come on."

I allow myself to be drug along, my eyes still flitting between a friend of old, and a new one. "Okay." More to myself than to my husband, "Tell me it's going to be okay."

A reassuring squeeze comes as we traverse the granules of sand, gaining on Edward. "It will be. This had to happen eventually. Shadow shouldn't hold a grudge forever."

Edward stops about fifteen feet away from Shadow, who just stares empty-faced. No emotions cross her features as she takes him in, and he does the same in turn. Shadow looks him up and down a few times, like she's looking for...a weapon.

Derk and I get closer, about five feet from Edward before Derk speaks carefully, gently, "Shadow, I'd like you to officially meet Edward."

Right away I notice how he had taken it, this official awkward introduction, away from being my fault. He was assuming responsibility for Edward, not me. I understand that was his way of trying to preserve any good standing I had with my old friend. My hand squeezes his in thanks, but my eyes are still on the two before me.

Edward puts his hand out, ready to shake Shadow's.

She looks at me, but emotion flicks across her face. Fear. But then it's gone, and so are her eyes as she looks back to Edward. When she speaks, it is quiet, but filled with distrust, "I know about you, Edward. How much *trouble* you were there."

"Trouble," Edward echoes as he looks down. "I...won't deny I've...caused problems. But I can honestly say I never went looking for trouble." He still has his hand out, and finally looks up. "I don't know how I got here, but I am grateful for Rebecca and Derk. I didn't have many friends back where I came from. In fact, I probably have none. I don't want any trouble. But more friends I would definitely take." His hand wavers a little. "Hi. I'm Edward."

She just looks at it, then over his shoulder to the weird water behind us. "They did this to her because of you, you know. It's affecting all of us. You are." Her eyes stay on the water.

Edward drops his hand and looks back at the water. "I'm...I'm sorry. I didn't know...this...any of this...didn't know. I'm sorry." With that, Edward turns and starts walking away in the direction of his little remade cabin.

Shadow calls out after him, eyes still on the water, "If you were really sorry, you'd help her."

Edward pauses, does a head bob in affirmation, and then turns around. "I would if I could. Rebecca told me the energy brought me here. We don't know how, or why. I'd go back and tear that place apart if I could."

Shadow nods, then looks at him. "Maybe that's why you're here then. So you don't tear it all apart. She did that once, and look what that did." She sighed loudly, "Nothing. Maybe you're supposed to get yourself all back together the right way, with no more...hostility...no more trouble. Then, maybe we can help *her*."

Tears well, then spill out of my eyes. *Oh Shadow!*

She looks at my face. *I still don't trust him.*

I know. But I do.

So...she's still trapped. Still drugged. And he's free. And you're okay with that?

Yes...because she helped him. The energy helped him.

"Hello," Derk snaps, "Still here! Still listening to silent dialog!".

She rolls her eyes and snaps, "Private conversation!"

Derk smirks, "Think I liked her better when she wasn't talking."

Edward walks over to us, "But she has a point. I need to control my anger about what was done to me. She did, and somehow got me here. Somehow, I have to repay that favor."

Shadow reaches out, "Hi. I'm Rebecca's best friend, Shadow Danza-Froste. And I do mean her best friend. So, now that you said you want to help her, that means you're in actuality, helping me." Edward shakes her hand gingerly. She holds his look, "I mean it. I'm her best friend, in any world, I take things personally."

"Obviously," Edward offers with a little smile.

Derk claps his hands together. "Well, that's great. Intros are over. People are talking. And I'm starving! Who's hungry?"

Together the four of us head to my place. Shadow tells me she'll take a rain check, until she can explain things over with her husband. I understand, and I think Derk does too. But, I admit aloud, how nice it will be to be all together again.

Shadow pauses, "That will be when we are *all together* again."

Chris gently turns Rebecca's drugged form over as

Corrine wipes her body down. The cocoon had wilted away after only a few months, so they had moved her to a different room, one with a window. Corrine had insisted on it, swearing it helped keep track of time passing and weather and nature and all that nonsense. She had won. So, sponge baths to help clean away dead skin were done by Corrine who had been angered by this "abhorrent treatment of a human being." To combat atrophy, electro shock treatments were administered and Chris and Corrine took turns moving the prone figure's limp limbs.

No spikes for Rebecca at any time over the past two-and-a-half years.

Corrine and her brother took to reading to Rebecca's sleeping form, as if she could hear them. Corrine even had her brother and Chris hold Rebecca up long enough for her to cut her hair, which had matted. Corrine insisted on combing it every few days and then settled on braiding it. She had felt it was a better way to keep the hair manageable.

Chris reaches out and touches the end of the braid. "Corrine, you're going to have to cut another few inches off."

Corrine nods solemnly as she continues to gently scrub the pale skin before her. "Ok."

Chris lets his eyes wander to the window as he looks away while Corrine cleans more personal areas. A sparrow sits on a branch outside the window. It hops closer to the window on its branch, like it can see him. Chris wonders what kind of views it sees, especially as it peeks inside today. He watches as it flitters to the window sill.

Rebecca twitches.

Chris adjusts his hold, as he has done before. He's grown accustomed to the small muscles spasms that periodically work through her body when being cleaned, after shock treatment, or when he's just sitting in the room with her. Seeing Corrine going back to work, he looks back out the window again.

The sparrow is still on the ledge. It's looking in. As Chris watches, it starts twitching.

So does Rebecca.

Chris looks quickly between the woman he's holding and the bird. The bird, falls to its side, tries to straighten, then falls from the ledge.

Rebecca stays still.

"All done," Corrine stands up to stretch her back. "Let me go get the scissors."

Chris lays his baggage down, situates the gown, sheet, and blanket.

His eyes go back to the window. Curiosity makes him get up and look out, then down.

The sparrow lay dead with other bird carcasses beneath the sill.

Bureau of Federal Energy and Interest   NRG-ASE

Case #: R00013ASE   Case Name: Rebecca
DOB: 07/23/1974   Code: energy

CLASSIFIED

Observation time/date: 28 December 2010/0723hrs
Report type: follow-up, monthly check-in
Time in observation: 802 days
Weight: 108lbs
Status: drug-induced coma

Notes:

Rebecca (Case #: R00013ASE) continues to be suspended in drug-induced coma. No energy spikes recorded. Physical therapy and sponge baths continue daily under supervision of Roberts.

Bureau of Federal Energy and Interest

DD Form 99-ASE   BFEI-USA   Subject Record

Bureau of Federal Energy and Interest   NRG-ASE

Case #: R00013ASE   Case Name: Rebecca
DOB: 07/23/1974   Code: energy

CLASSIFIED

Observation time/date: 8 January 2012/0838hrs
Report type: follow-up, bi-monhly
Time in observation: 11788 days
Weight: 102lbs
Status: drug-induced coma

Notes:

Rebecca (Case #: R00013ASE) continues to be suspended in drug-induced coma. No energy spikes recorded. Physical therapy and sponge baths continue daily under supervision of Roberts.

Corrine suggests taking subject out of coma, sixth time. Roberts agrees.

Bureau of Federal Energy and Interest

DD Form 99-ASE   BFEI-USA   Subject Record

CHAPTER 40

Edward zones in on me. He's getting so good at this, this finding me no matter the distance between our bodies. For the past year we've really gotten to know each other. More importantly, he's come to know the energy around us. How it asks, listening to what it wants, and what it can do. He's been humbled, but empowered. He's now a match for me.

Together we have been working hard, searching hard, for her.

And we did.

The link was so very faint, we missed it how many times. Way too many. About five months of working with Edward to catch him up to me, as Shadow says, we started feeling for any signs or ties to her. I walked paths once familiar. Took new ones. I had even gone into the water, submerged myself until I thought I had passed on, but to no avail.

It was the birds. Why they weren't obvious is tricky. For two years, no birds, no singing, right? But it was one day as Shadow and I were taking Rebecca Jo through the woods towards Edward's cabin, and I saw a fresh, clean but frayed brown feather. I didn't see the bird, didn't hear it. Soon, I realized, there were other feathers scattered about. I related this finding to Shadow and Derk, talked with them about before Edward had crossed and the path where it was silent, where something was wrong.

Looking back, I feel like an idiot. I should have known, been more observant.

Edward found the first bird. It was...weird, like stunned, in an upper branch of a tree. So weak, I almost thought it was dead.

The energy told us otherwise. It linked us, the bird limp in Edward's hand and me. It had startled me at first, I admit, but so life changing. I felt, heard things, heard song, felt the breeze, and something else. It was...powerful in that little limp form. I cannot even begin to explain it fully beyond,...I had my senses back in that moment, all of them. Then it died.

We went bird hunting. No, hunting isn't quite right. We went bird searching, to find and acquire what we could. Three months, eight birds, all the same, limp, but giving us our senses back more fully.

Sadly, all eight birds perished after these "power transfers," as Edward calls them. I felt a loss with each passing, and wept.

Today, there was something different. It started as a dot, moving across the horizon. I thought it was my eyes playing tricks on me. But Shadow and Edward saw it too, especially as it got closer. And it did. The closer it got, the weaker it looked. Tired, like it had traversed a terrific distance. After about thirty minutes, it was upon us. A single black feather fell, and then the crow did, just before me.

Ready? Edward whispered to me as we join with it's dying force.

Are you there?

I had jumped back and recoiled. It was her voice, from three years before. So weak, Edward had assumed it was an echo of my mind, but I quickly latched onto her signal,...failing with every rise and fall of the crow's chest. "Yes!" I know I had said it aloud and mentally, because everyone looked at me.

Help me.

And the crow died.

But Edward had followed my link, felt the trail left behind. He had smiled. "And so we will."

Chris gently turns Rebecca's drugged form over for the umpteenth umpteenth time, but this one will be different. Carefully he pulls the monitors off her back, and the machines go haywire for the span of time it takes for him to lay her back down and shut them off. He pulls up her blankets, to her ears, like she used to, and waits in "his chair."

He had seen a crow outside her window today. Like so many other birds that had come up to peer inside, it had twitched, Rebecca along with it, then fallen to its death. Chris had mentioned this phenomenon to Corrine, who had shrugged him off the first few times. Now she was a believer. Over thirty dead birds had piled up outside her room's window in the past few months. Security thought there must have been a rogue electrical charge that goes out every so often, bringing the birds to their demise. But Chris and Corrine had a different opinion on the matter.

Today it would be tested.

It has been over three years since they sedated her with her last spike. That had been the day after Edward had gone missing. No sign of Edward, anywhere. At any time. No spikes for Rebecca either in that time. So it had been decided to bring her about, and pretend that time hadn't moved on without her knowledge.

Chris wasn't sure she was going to buy it. Roberts had definitely more age lines, and had given Chris more gray hair. Maybe, being inside wouldn't give away how much time had passed. But his patience had wore too think. But this is what Chris was signed up to do. He was to be a part of the agency, be there as they needed him. That was his job.

But, now...this was a whole new ballgame. There were new players on the field.

The monitors being to register a stronger heartbeat. Chris smiles a bit. Last time they had had her out for about three weeks. Not three years. He doubted any vomit would hit his pants this time.

whispers...

silence...

        fluttery feeling...

light...   then darkness...

    a voice...

again...

                a hand...

machines beeping...

    Chris's drawl...

    Chris's voice again...with a hand at my brow...

    My eyes open. They flutter closed.

    Silence.

But Chris won't let me rest. "Rebecca, come on. You've slept enough."

Chris stays with me until my nausea subsides, and my muscles remember how to move. And I don't know if I want to open my eyes.

Did you enjoy this book?

The journey starts with:

Another Day

and continues with:

Another Place
Another One

Take a different adventure:

Illness

Follow me on Facebook:-
http://www.facebook.com/jodiemswanson

Twitter:-
http://www.twitter.com/jodiemswanson

JODIE M. SWANSON

Made in the USA
Lexington, KY
16 June 2017